Romance at the Christmas Tree Lot

Marcia Lynn McClure

Published by Distractions Ink
1290 Mirador Loop N.E.
Rio Rancho, NM 87144

Published by Distractions Ink
©Copyright 2014 by M. Meyers
A.K.A. Marcia Lynn McClure
Cover Photography by © /Jason Hipp/Dreamstime.com and
Cover Design and Interior Graphics
by Sandy Ann Allred/Timeless Allure

First Printed Edition: December 2014

McClure, Marcia Lynn, 1965—
Romance at the Christmas Tree Lot a novella/by Marcia Lynn
McClure.

ISBN: 978-0-9913878-9-2

Library of Congress Control Number: 2014959487

Printed in the United States of America

To All of Us...

To help us savor the sweet, sublime, yet simple peace
that the very existence of Christmas offers to our
hearts and souls and that true love is not to be
doubted—whether instantaneously known or slowly
discovered. Merry Christmas!

CHAPTER ONE

"Mmmm!" Mayvee sighed with contentment. She took another sip of hot chocolate from the red and white mug she held. Glancing around the room inside the small, rustic-looking building, she smiled. Everything had come together as smoothly as it ever had—even with her dad being away on deployment.

Mayvee straightened the stacks of white Styrofoam cups sitting near the hot chocolate dispensing machine. The napkin dispenser was full, and several jars filled with soft peppermint sticks were waiting to be used as hot chocolate stirrers.

"Hot chocolate station…check," Mayvee mumbled to herself. Savoring another sip of the warm, sweet beverage in the mug she held, Mayvee stepped aside to inspect the cookie table. Sugar cookies decorated with white frosting and colored sugar sprinkles sat stacked on Christmas-themed serving platters, each platter accompanied by a small pile of little snack napkins. "Cookies…check," Mayvee said. She nodded toward the cash register sitting on the counter nearby and, speaking directly to it as if it were a living thing, said, "And you're all plugged in and working too."

She looked around her again, dazzled a bit by how beautiful the inside of the little sales shed was—white icicle lights fairly dripping from the rafters and pine boughs, strung with white lights, edging the room where the walls met the ceiling.

Oh sure, Mayvee Ashton had grown up spending every December at her family's Christmas tree lot. Still, the excitement of the Christmas season, and the beauty of the Christmas tree lot and its small sales center, never failed to send a thrill of delight and excited anticipation racing through her.

Stepping out of the sales center and into the crisp afternoon air, Mayvee relished the rich, invigorating scent of pine. The tip of her nose tingled with just the right amount of Jack Frost's nipping, and as Doris Day's sweet and vintage rendition of "Christmas Story" begin to waft from the sound system out over the tree lot world, Mayvee again sighed with satisfaction.

Indeed, everything at Ashtons' Christmas Tree Lot looked perfectly festive and welcoming. From the outside of the sales center, slathered in colored lights and dripping with silver icicles, to the roped off pre-cut tree area, to the cut-your-own-tree field of a variety of pines beyond—everything was primed and ready for opening night.

"Well, it looks like we're finally ready," Mayvee's older brother, Craig, said as he walked toward her through the trees in the pre-cut area. He smiled, raked a hand back through his dark hair, and added, "Dad will be proud of us for doing such a good job."

"He totally will," Mayvee agreed. The familiar ache of missing her father crunched her heart a moment in thinking of him—in missing him. "I think the trees miss him though," she said, trying to will away the heartache of separation.

"Me too," Craig said, smiling at Mayvee with understanding. He nodded toward her mug of still-steaming hot chocolate. "Can I have a swig?"

"Of course," Mayvee answered, handing the mug to her brother.

"Mmm," Craig hummed with approval. "It's as good as ever." He took another swig. "I'm always kind of tired of it by the end of the season every year, thinking that it won't taste as good come the next year. But it always does."

Mayvee giggled. "That's one of the magical things about Christmas," she said. "So many things taste better, look better, feel better during the holidays. People love more, give more, think more about others, you know?" She sighed. "I wish everyone could just carry those feelings with them all through the year. I mean, what's the point of celebrating the birth of the Savior if you don't appreciate his birth the rest of the year, you know?"

"Yeah, I do know," Craig agreed.

"Okay! It's working fine!" Josh called as he jogged over from the direction of the Christmas tree baling machine. "I've put that first roll of netting on and tried it out, and it's all good."

"Awesome," Craig said. "Man! Do you remember the days before Dad hooked us up with the baler, Josh?"

"Not really," Josh admitted.

"I do," Mayvee sighed. "We were always so covered in sap, and our hands were raw from tying trees to cars. I'm still so full from Thanksgiving dinner yesterday that I can't even imagine having to go back to selling Christmas trees today without it. I love the baler!"

"You mean the pooper," Josh chuckled.

Craig and Mayvee laughed too, but Craig still reminded their younger brother, "Just don't let the customers hear us calling it that."

"I know," Josh said, scowling. "What? Do you think I'm an idiot?"

Craig and Mayvee exchanged understanding glances.

"Of course not," Mayvee assured her little brother. "It's just when I was sixteen like you, one of the customers heard me call it the tree pooper, and she got all mad and threw a hissy fit at Dad."

"Ooo! I remember that," Craig moaned. "Old Mrs. Mushbottom! She was so mean. I almost didn't feel bad when she passed away."

Trying not to laugh but failing, Mayvee said, "Her name was Mrs. Sushraddum, Craig…and you know it."

Craig grinned, winked at his sister, and said, "Mushbottom, Sushraddum…whatever. She was cranky."

"I know she was," Mayvee admitted. "But she was—"

"A widow," Craig interrupted. "Yeah, I know. A poor little old widow, spending Christmases alone. I get

4

that, and I felt bad for her too. But grandma always told us that a person catches more flies with honey than vinegar, and Mrs. Mushbottom was so vinegar, you know? So I always think of her as Mrs. Mushbottom—because at least calling her that makes me remember her more fondly."

"Okay, so don't call the tree pooper the tree pooper in front of customers. Got it," Josh said, rolling his blue eyes with exasperation. "I swear, this family has the hardest time staying on topic sometimes."

Mayvee smiled with amusement. Josh was right; the entire Ashton family could slide off topic faster than anything.

"Go get some hot chocolate, Josh," Mayvee suggested. "It's perfect this year, and it will warm you up so you're ready to poop trees when the lot opens." She reached up, tousling his brown hair as if he were still a toddler.

"Knock it off, Mayvee," Josh teased. He ran a hand through his hair to straighten it. "I mean, what if a group of hot babes come by to pick out a tree? I gotta look suave."

"Oh yeah," Mayvee giggled. "I forgot how many sixteen-year-old hot babes come Christmas tree shopping in groups…without their parents."

But Josh smiled and shrugged. "It could happen." He reached out then, tugging on the two long blonde braids that hung out from under Mayvee's stocking cap on either side of her head. "And maybe Dagwood Bumstead will drop in and propose, Blondie."

Mayvee's pretty light brown eyebrows wrinkled quizzically. "What? Who's Dagwood Bumstead?"

"The sandwich guy, Mayvee. Remember?" Craig offered. "From that old comic strip *Blondie*? The one Grandpa just *had* to read every Sunday? The guy the Dagwood sandwich is named after?"

"Oh yeah...the guy that's always running into the postman on his way to work," Mayvee said, finally toppling to the meaning of Josh's teasing. Snatching her braid from her little brother's hold, she said, "Well, I wouldn't marry a man named after a sandwich...even if he did show up at our tree lot."

Craig laughed as Josh corrected, "No, no, Blondie. The sandwich was named after Dagwood."

"All the same," Mayvee began, "I couldn't marry a Dagwood. How would that sound? 'Dagwood, honey, would you take the trash out for me?'" Continuing to speak in an high-pitched, alternate voice, Mayvee positioned her hand so that her thumb was at her ear and her pinky at her mouth to simulate a phone and continued, "'Hi, Mom. Can Dagwood and I drop by for a sandwich? Oh, Dagwood and I are so excited for the new baby! I think we'll call it Reuben if it's a boy and Pattymelt if it's a girl.'" With both Craig and Josh smiling with amusement, Mayvee finished, "Nope. Dagwood isn't for me."

"Oh, come on, Mayvee," Craig chuckled. "I mean, after you have two kids named Reuben and Pattymelt, you might as well have s'more!"

As Josh and Craig erupted into laugher, Mayvee, although giggling as well, shook her head and said, "You guys think you're so funny."

"S'more! Good one, man!" Josh laughed as he and Craig bumped knuckles with triumph.

"Hey, guys! Sorry I'm late," Rhonda Ashton said as she hurried toward her three children who stood laughing among the pines. "I had to stop and pick up some more cups and napkins." Rhonda paused, studying her children a moment. "What did I miss?"

"Stupidity," Mayvee answered as she hugged her mother and placed a welcoming kiss on her cheek.

"Stupidity?" Craig countered. "You mean awesomeness!"

Mayvee rolled her eyes as Craig kissed his mother's cheek.

"Hi, Mom," Josh greeted, also kissing her cheek. "I've got the tree pooper all set up, working, and ready to rock."

Rhonda sighed with relief. "Oh good!" she said. "Let's hope it gets a lot of use this year, hmmm?"

"It will, Mom," Craig reassured her.

Mayvee felt so sorry for her mother. This would be the first year they'd ever had to run the Christmas tree lot without her father. Keith Ashton's deployment to Afghanistan wouldn't end until after Christmas. It would be his very last deployment—for he was retiring from a long, decorated military career upon his return—but for some reason, Mayvee's father's final deployment had been the hardest ever on his wife and children. Mayvee could see the near constant worry in her mother's eyes and desperately wished there were some way she could soothe it.

Still, she knew the Christmas tree lot would keep her mother busy through the season—and that would distract her from her worries a little at least. It would somewhat distract them all, and Mayvee was thankful for it.

♥

Black Friday—it was an appalling phrase. At least Kord's mother thought it was. Kord's father was a history professor, and therefore, Kord knew enough about the history of where Black Friday got its name for it to leave a bad taste in his mouth. It never failed that, on the Friday following Thanksgiving Day, his mom would firmly yet kindly make sure that her children understood that in her opinion, Black Friday was in total opposition to what the beginning of the season marking the celebration of the birth of Christ should be.

Kord's dad had explained years before that Black Friday—a term coined by overworked, frustrated policemen in the mid-1960s—was a phrase aptly applied to describe the madness of massive traffic jams, mob-like throngs of pedestrians, and basically utter chaos that had ensued every Friday following Thanksgiving Day since the mid-1920s. Kord's mother thought it not only ironic but also morally inappropriate that Americans would spend the fourth Thursday of every November in giving humble thanks to their Maker, only to begin the celebration of his Son's birth by lurching out the next morning to participate in a competitive race to spend money. Of course, Kord knew some truly did see Black Friday as an opportunity to begin sincere celebration of the Christmas season—to thoughtfully purchase gifts for family and friends, to be given with the utmost sincerity in love. But it was the other faction—the selfish, crazy, often angry and mean shoppers—that had driven Kord's mom to set the day after Thanksgiving as a day when the Derringer family stayed at home to play board games, drink warm cider, eat leftover turkey and pumpkin pie, and enjoy one or two traditional Christmas movies together in the evening. As a result, having spent each and every Black Friday of his growing-up years in a warm, comfortable, and peaceful atmosphere at home, Kord would much rather have just slept through the chaotic day rather than step foot out of his house. But his job was necessary, of course, so each Black Friday, he'd go to work in the morning as if it were any other day of the workweek. However, when work was finished, he'd head directly back home, without stopping for so much as a tank of gas.

But this year was different. This year, there was one important purchase Kord absolutely *needed* to make on Black Friday—a Christmas tree for his grandpa and grandma. And so, as he pulled into the parking lot of Ashtons' Christmas Tree Lot, Kord inhaled a deep breath of determination to complete his errand as quickly and painlessly as possible.

Consequently, because Kord was somewhere other than home on the evening of Black Friday, he was reminded of just how much he loved and cared for his grandma and grandpa. His grandma needed her Christmas tree, and his grandpa wasn't able to go out to get one for her. Therefore, Kord had offered to procure a fresh-cut tree for them both. So there he was—out and about on Black Friday, striding toward the tree lot.

Oddly enough, the closer Kord drew to the entrance of Ashtons' Christmas Tree Lot, the less anxious he became about being out on Black Friday and the more eager he became for the Christmas season. For one thing, he could almost hear the instructions his grandma had given to him as he was leaving the house.

"Be sure you get one at least seven feet tall, Kord honey," she'd said. "And make sure it's full enough to fill up that space in our bay window."

Kord smiled as he thought of his grandma—of all the Christmas Eves spent in her kitchen and around the tree that his grandma and grandpa had always hunted for, brought home, put up, and decorated. To Kord, his grandparents were as much a part of the fun part of the season as were candy canes, sugar cookies, Santa Claus, and watching Frank Capra's *It's a Wonderful Life*.

But it wasn't just thoughts of his grandma and grandpa that lifted his spirits and drove away his "Mom's right" concerns about the world's chaos on Black Friday: it was the way the sight of the Christmas tree lot drew him in, as if he were about to step out of the mucky stress of life and right into some mythical forest—a forest dripping with the scent of pine and peppermint and covered in colored lights and tinsel.

"Well, I think we can quit holding our breath," Rhonda Ashton said to her daughter. "Looks like opening night is going to be a success."

"It sure does," Mayvee assured her mother. "Whenever Thanksgiving falls on the last Thursday of November, it seems people know they're gonna be short on time, and they tend to get busy getting their tree up before things get too crazy with shopping and shipping and stuff."

"Thank goodness," Rhonda sighed. She shook her head for a moment. "Every year, your dad and I worry that the tree lot won't be able to pay for itself, you know? But if tonight is any indication, it will this year."

Mayvee smiled at her mom and put her arm around her shoulders. "It certainly will." She glanced in the direction of the baler. "It looks like Josh is feeding trees through the baler faster than green grass through a goose."

Rhonda laughed. "Yep. He loves working that stupid baler, doesn't he?"

"I do too, actually," Mayvee explained. "It's a lot of fun, not to mention the aggravation it saves for us and the customer."

"Well, good evening, ladies."

Mayvee and her mother both turned to see a familiar face attached to the familiar voice that had spoken.

"Good evening, Mr. Swanson!" Rhonda greeted, offering the elderly man her hand. "It's so good to see you out tonight." She looked past him, asking, "Where's Edna?"

But Mr. Swanson exhaled a heavy sigh, shook his head, and answered, "Poor girl broke a hip a couple of weeks ago, so she sent me on my own this year."

"Oh dear!" Rhonda exclaimed with genuine concern. "Poor Edna! Are you two holding up okay? Do you need anything?"

"Oh, goodness sakes, no," Mr. Swanson assured her. "We're plugging along just fine. I just need a tree." He paused, glanced to Mayvee, and added, "And to sign up to have someone decorate it for me."

A pang of worry and sadness pricked at Mayvee's heart at this news. Mr. and Mrs. Swanson were getting quite old, and she knew that the day would come when they wouldn't be visiting the tree lot, together or individually.

Still, she linked an arm through his, forced a smile, and responded, "Well, we'll have to be sure we find one that pleases her then, won't we? And I have my entire decorating schedule open tomorrow, so name your time, and I'll be there!"

Mr. Swanson smiled, his countenance brightening with hope and reassurance. "Oh good!" he chuckled. "Ever since you started decorating our tree for us, Edna enjoys the whole season so much more because she can just sit and admire the tree...instead of having to do all the work herself."

"Well, you tell Mrs. Swanson that I'll be over tomorrow. And by the time I'm finished, her tree will be swimming in colored lights and shiny ornaments and dripping with icicles!"

Mr. Swanson chuckled again, patted Mayvee's hand where it rested at the crook of his arm, and said, "Oh, she'll be so glad to hear that. Indeed, she will."

"It looks like you're in good hands with Mayvee, Mr. Swanson," Rhonda said as another customer waved, indicating he needed her assistance. "Merry Christmas! And send Edna my love."

"I sure will," Mr. Swanson said. "Now, what kinds of trees do you Ashtons have this year?"

"Oh, so many kinds!" Mayvee answered with an excited giggle. "And I'll decorate your tree for free, of course, Mr. Swanson," Mayvee added, "as my Christmas gift to you."

"Oh no, you won't!" Mr. Swanson argued, however. "I'll pay you whatever your hourly wage is this year. You've gotta eat, after all."

Mayvee smiled at him, and not wanting to hurt his pride (for she knew how important it was to elderly people to remain in control of the things that they could), she said, "Okay. We'll work that out after we've found your tree."

"That sounds perfect," Mr. Swanson agreed, again patting the back of Mayvee's hand.

"Wanna start with the white firs like last year?" Mayvee asked. "Or do you think Mrs. Swanson would want a noble fir this year?"

Mr. Swanson's bushy gray brows puckered. "I don't quite know," he admitted. "But she did like the tree we had last year. She said it was one of her favorites, and I think it was a white fir."

"It was indeed," Maybe confirmed. "I love nobles too, but it's more difficult to put the lights and ornaments all the way inside the tree. White firs are so perfect for that."

"Let's look at white firs then, Mayvee," Mr. Swanson concluded.

Mayvee giggled, tightened her grip on Mr. Swanson's arm, and said, "Right this way then, Mr. Swanson. We'll find a tree that'll make Mrs. Swanson's eyes bug out!"

Mr. Swanson laughed, "Ha ha! What a sight that would be!"

Mayvee smiled as she led Mr. Swanson toward the section of the lot stocked with pre-cut white fir trees. She'd make sure Mrs. Swanson had the perfect tree for her home—one that Mayvee could decorate just the way Mrs. Swanson wanted.

Kord felt a smile tug at the corners of his mouth as he studied the young woman helping the elderly man choose a Christmas tree. She was a very pretty blonde, wearing a pair of very well-worn jeans, a set of work boots, and a red sweatshirt. The sweatshirt was embellished with a large image of Santa on the front, captioned by the phrase, *I believe!* Kord chuckled a little to himself, noting that the knitted blue, gray, and maroon striped stocking cap the young woman wore looked just like the one worn by Ralphie's little brother, Randy, in the classic movie *A Christmas Story*.

The tree lot girl's long flax-colored hair hung in two braids on either side of her head, peeking out from under her stocking cap to give her a confident, carefree appearance. She reached back, pulling a pair of tattered work gloves from the back pocket of her jeans and pulled them on to protect soft-looking hands, as she reached into the tree the elderly man was pointing to.

"Oh, this is a beautiful tree, Mr. Swanson!" Kord heard the young woman exclaim. "It will look just perfect in your front window."

Kord's smile broadened. The girl's voice was cute— sort of femininely squeaky with excitement, as if there were a giggle waiting at the end of each word she spoke.

"I think so," the old man said, "though I wish Edna were here to confirm it."

The tree lot girl's expression saddened as she reached out and grasped one of the old man's hands in her free one. "I know," she said, her voice suddenly owning a soothing intonation. "But I'll be by tomorrow to decorate it for you, and maybe next year Mrs. Swanson will be up to coming along to choose the tree. Hmmm?"

The old man smiled. "You're right, Mayvee," the man agreed. "After all, any old bough of pine will look stunning after you've dressed it up."

The young woman (obviously named Mayvee) giggled, kissed the old man on the cheek, and said, "Flattery will get you everywhere, Mr. Swanson!" Taking hold of the Christmas tree the man had chosen, the tree lot girl seemed to have no problem whatsoever rocking it back and forth until the trunk (which had been securely buried in the lot's loose dirt) gave way so she could pull the tree aside.

"Now, I'll just have Josh saw about…oh, let's say six inches off the trunk's bottom, send it through the tree baler to net it for you, and toss it in the back of your pickup."

"Oh, Mayvee, you don't have do all that," Mr. Swanson began.

But the girl smiled and said, "Oh, I'm not going to do it. Josh will!" She laughed, turned her head toward the small outbuilding nearby, and, in her cute, squeaky voice, called, "Josh! I need you to finish taking care of Mr. Swanson's tree for me!" She then turned her attention back to the old man, smiled, and said, "And I'll see you and Mrs. Swanson at about eleven a.m. tomorrow morning to get the tree all decorated for ya.

Okay?" She paused, adding, "Though…I do wish you'd just let me do the decorating for free…as my Christmas gift to you and Mrs. Swanson."

The old man shook his head, however, emphatically countering, "No. No, we'll pay you to decorate it just like we do every year. It's worth far more than the cost, Mayvee. We old folks just don't have the energy necessary to do the tree anymore." He smiled. "And besides, you've got bills to pay, don't you? It's why you offer the decorating service, isn't it?"

The young woman blushed a little and nodded. "Well, it's one reason, anyway," she admitted. "But it's different for you and Mrs. Swanson. I just don't feel right about—"

"That's enough," the man kindly interrupted. "Now get your brother to feed that tree through the baler and heft it into my truck, and Edna and I will see you tomorrow morning, okay?" He playfully wagged an index finger at the girl and said, "And that's the end of it."

The tree lot girl, Mayvee, laughed as a teenage boy looking to be about fifteen or sixteen arrived and took the tree from her.

"Thanks, Josh," she said to the boy.

"I'll have this netted for you in just a second, Mr. Swanson," the boy said.

"Thank you, Josh," Mr. Swanson said.

Mayvee waved as the old man began to follow the kid carrying his tree toward the back of the lot. "Tell Mrs. Swanson that I'm just dying to have some of her toffee when I get there, okay?" she called.

Mr. Swanson nodded and chuckling said, "Oh, she made a fresh batch just yesterday because she knew I'd be scheduling you to come by to decorate the tree tomorrow. So you can have your fill of toffee."

"Can I help you, sir?" someone asked, stepping up next to Kord.

Reluctant to take his attention off the tree lot girl, Kord looked to his right to see a tall guy looking to be about his own age standing next to him.

"If you're the man I see about buying a Christmas tree, then yes," Kord answered, offering a friendly smile.

"Awesome! Craig Ashton," the man said, offering a gloved hand to Kord.

"Kord Derringer," Kord said, grasping Craig's hand in a firm handshake.

"Are you looking to cut your own tree, Kord?" Craig asked. "Or did you want to grab one that's already cut?"

"Actually, I'm just picking up a tree for my grandparents this year," Kord began. "And did I hear someone say you guys provide a tree-decorating service too?"

"Yeah, we do," Craig confirmed. "Did you want to schedule a time for someone to come out and decorate it for your grandparents?"

"That would be incredibly helpful…so yeah," Kord answered.

"Awesome," Craig said. "My mom and sister both provide the decorating service, so depending on—"

"Is the cute blonde with the pigtails your sister then?" Kord couldn't help interrupting.

Craig grinned with understanding. "Indeed she is…and she's awesome with decorating trees."

"Cool," Kord said. "I was watching her help out an old man a minute ago. She seems good with elderly people."

"Oh, she is," Craig confirmed. He chuckled, adding, "And to save you the awkwardness of having to ask, she's single and conveniently unattached at the moment too."

"Oh. I'm not a creeper or anything like that, man," Kord began, realizing that the tree lot guy had assumed Kord was interested in his sister—which he was. But he didn't want her brother thinking he was a psycho or anything. "I just heard her talking to that old guy and thought she'd probably do well with my grandparents. And my grandma isn't up to decorating her own tree this year, so—"

But Craig Ashton smiled, slapped Kord on the shoulder, and called, "Mayvee! We gotta customer needing a tree for his grandma."

Kord felt his face go red with embarrassment. "Dude," he began, shaking his head at Craig.

"She's really good with older people, man. No worries," Craig assured him. "Seriously, she'll do a great job for your grandma and grandpa."

"Yeah?" the tree lot girl asked as she hurried over to where Kord stood talking to her brother.

"This gentleman is in the market for a tree for his grandparents *and* a decorator to bling it up for them," Craig explained to his sister. "He says his name is Dagwood."

Kord's brows puckered with confusion as he offered his hand to the tree lot girl and said, "Um…my name's Kord, actually."

The pretty blonde shook his hand and playfully scowled at her brother for a moment, before smiling her pretty smile at Kord. He noticed that her beautiful green-blue eyes twinkled as she looked at him—like they had tiny stars trapped inside them or something.

"I'm Mayvee," she said in the perfectly feminine voice that hinted at barely restrained giggles. "So you're looking for a tree for your grandparents?"

"Yeah," Kord answered. He hoped it didn't show—the fact that he was entirely captivated by her, a girl he'd only just met. "My grandma had knee-replacement surgery a couple of weeks ago, and my grandpa has to use a walker…so I'm their Christmas tree guy this year."

"Oh, how cute!" Mayvee exclaimed—and this time she did indeed giggle after speaking. "They are so lucky to have such a goodhearted grandson."

"Well, I leave you to Mayvee's masterful skills in selecting Christmas trees for grandmothers," Craig said. "Nice to meet you, and Merry Christmas, man."

"Merry Christmas," Kord returned, trying to remember the last time he'd heard a guy his age tell anyone merry Christmas.

"So, Kord," Mayvee began. Kord grinned with amusement and pleasure as Mayvee linked her arm through the crook of his just the way he'd seen her do with the elderly man she'd been helping before. "What kind of tree does your grandma like?"

Kord shrugged. "I'm not sure," he answered. "She just told me to make sure it was at least seven feet tall and full enough to fill her bay window area. She didn't specify a species or whatever."

Mayvee giggled. "Oh, I see. Well, what kinds of ornaments does she like to hang on her tree? Big ones, small ones, all kinds?"

Kord smiled then; *that* he knew. "Oh yeah, she has a ton of those glass ornaments by that famous glass ornament guy," he said. "You know, the ones that some of them are nice looking and others are kind of creepy. Do you know the ones I mean?"

Mayvee laughed again. "I totally do. You mean Christopher Radko ornaments, right?"

"Yeah! That's the guy!" Kord exclaimed. "My grandma has a lot of those Radko ornaments—the pretty ones, not the ugly ones."

Mayvee couldn't keep from giggling. The fact that this tall, dark, and handsome Christmas tree shopper was at the lot to buy a Christmas tree for his grandparents was endearing enough on its own. But add to it the fact that he'd paid enough attention to his grandma's Christmas ornaments to know she liked Radko ornaments was just too adorable!

When Craig had called her over to help a new customer, Mayvee hadn't expected to see a guy so classically handsome that he looked like he'd stepped straight out of Hollywood's Silver Screen era. But at the same time, Kord was more rugged-looking than any truly manly-man she'd ever seen.

Not wanting the man to pick up on the fact that she found him dazzlingly attractive, Mayvee dove back into conversation. "Radko ornaments can be pretty heavy sometimes, so your grandma probably wants a sturdy tree that can take some weight. Maybe we should look at noble firs."

The man shrugged. "You'd know better than I would. And do you guys really provide a tree decorating service? Because that would be a really big help—if someone could help me put the tree up and get all the stuff on."

A wave of excitement raced through Mayvee at the idea that she might actually be able to see the hunk of eye candy again, so she eagerly exclaimed, "We do. In fact, I could help you with your grandma's tree myself! I'd love to see her Radko ornaments."

She heard a low chuckle rumble in Kord's broad chest. "Well then, how much do you charge?"

"Ten dollars an hour," Mayvee said. In truth, she usually charged fifteen to twenty an hour depending on the difficulty of the job. But for the chance to see Kord again—well, heck! She'd have done it for free!

"Great," Kord said, sighing with relief. "Do you have any openings tomorrow?"

"I do," Mayvee assured him. "But only after two. I have one other decorating commitment in the morning."

"Two would be perfect," Kord said.

Mayvee noted to herself that Kord's voice sounded something like she imagined a lumberjack's voice would—strong, confident, and low in intonation. She glanced up at him, suddenly struck silent by the bright blue-green of his eyes, his perfectly square chin, straight nose, dark eyelashes and eyebrows, and a smile that made her knees feel like they'd turned to applesauce.

"I…I guess we better find your grandma's tree first though, huh?" she stammered.

"Probably," Kord said, looking down at her. His knee-weakening smile broadened, having such an overwhelming effect on Mayvee's nervous system that she felt light-headed for a moment.

Suddenly very self-conscious, she realized how brazen she'd been by taking his arm the way she had Mr. Swanson's. It was a habit she'd formed when helping elderly people, for she found it added support and helped them feel more confident in walking through the rather uneven terrain of the tree lot, as well as warming them, both heart and body.

But the way she'd taken Kord's arm now seemed not only forward but also ridiculously assuming. Yet when she began to remove her arm from his, he chuckled and took hold of her hand to keep it in the crook of his arm.

"You wouldn't deny me the same friendly treatment I saw you giving that old guy a few minutes ago, would you?" Kord seemed to tease.

"I-I suppose not," Mayvee giggled nervously.

"Good," he said. "I usually don't go anywhere on Black Friday, except to work. So it helps me to have a pretty girl on my arm while I'm braving this wild crowd."

Mayvee smiled as she nodded toward the group of noble fir trees nearby. "Well, I'm glad I can be of assistance, Mr.…Mr.…" she prodded.

"Derringer," Kord offered. "Kord Derringer."

"Well, I'm glad I can be of assistance, Mr. Derringer," Mayvee began, "to *you* tonight and your *grandparents* tomorrow."

"Me too," he said—again flashing his bone-dissolving smile at her. His handsome brows puckered a minute, however, and he asked, "Why did your brother introduce me to you as Dagwood, anyway?"

Mayvee sighed, shook her head, and rolled her eyes. "Who knows?" she said with a shrug.

But Mayvee knew *exactly* why Craig had introduced Kord as Dagwood—to imply that she was Blondie from the archaic comic strip and that Dagwood (a.k.a. Kord Derringer) had shown up at the Christmas tree lot to propose to her.

"If only!" Mayvee exclaimed aloud in a whisper.

"What's that?" Kord asked.

But Mayvee just pointed straight ahead to a large, beautifully shaped noble fir. "There," she said. "That one looks to be about eight feet tall and really full at the bottom, not to mention being able to support your grandma's ornaments. What do you think?"

She heard Kord sigh with satisfaction. "I think I'm glad I braved the mania of Black Friday for the sake of my grandma and grandpa," he said.

"Me too," Mayvee again whispered to herself. "Oh, me too."

CHAPTER TWO

Mr. and Mrs. Swanson's tree had been a joy to decorate! Mayvee had eaten more than her fair share of Mrs. Swanson's incredible toffee during her time with them too. In fact, her stomach felt a bit out of whack from all the toffee she'd eaten while decorating their tree. At least she had assumed it was the excessive enjoyment of the toffee that had her stomach churning. But now, as she pulled up in front of the address Kord Derringer had given to her the night before, the unsettled feeling in her stomach increased, and she began to think that maybe it was nerves and not Mrs. Swanson's toffee that had her stomach flip-flopping.

The night before, after Kord had explained that he needed a tree for his grandparents and that he'd like for Mayvee to decorate it for them, Mayvee had helped him select a beautiful noble fir. Once Josh had chainsawed about five inches off the bottom of the trunk, he'd put it through the tree pooper and carried it to Kord Derringer's truck for him. Mayvee had walked with Josh and Kord to Kord's truck and smiled when Kord tipped Josh ten bucks for helping him with the tree.

Kord had then written down his grandparents' address, said that he would go ahead and string the lights on the tree the next morning, and told her he would look forward to seeing her that afternoon. Then he'd hopped in his big black pickup and driven away into the night.

Kord Derringer may have driven away from the Christmas tree lot, but he sure lingered in Mayvee's mind. In fact, he lingered there all night long—lingered so stalwartly that Mayvee had had a rough time sleeping because of the visions of Kord Derringer dancing in her head.

Dang, he was so good-looking. Tall, dark, and handsome, flirtatious, strong—not to mention a guy who cared for his grandparents, a man her grandmother would've referred to as a "real dreamboat!"

Therefore, as Mayvee parked her car in front of 307 North Plum Orchard, she admitted that the churning in her stomach was indeed due to nervous anticipation about seeing Kord again and not because she'd eaten too much of Edna Swanson's toffee.

Mayvee retrieved her bag of extra decorating supplies from the trunk of her car and headed up the quaint little walkway leading to the old but well-kept house. She smiled as she ascended the few steps leading up to the front porch because the house looked just like a grandma's house should look—small, vintage, bright, and clean, with a beautiful Christmas wreath made of fresh pine boughs and red velvet ribbon already hanging on the front door to greet visitors.

Inhaling a breath of courage and thinking of the *Sound of Music* at the moment Maria reaches the front door of Captain Von Trapp's house and starts to lose her confidence, Mayvee reached out and pushed the doorbell button. The sound of Westminster chimes on the other side of the door did nothing to boost her nerve, and she clutched her supplies bag with both hands and smiled as she waited for the door to open.

She hadn't realized she'd been holding her breath with anxiety until the door swung in and she saw Kord standing just inside, smiling at her.

"Hi," he greeted with a handsome, very friendly smile.

"Hi," Mayvee responded as she exhaled her tightly held breath. She blushed a little, knowing that her response probably sounded like a sigh of admiration.

But Kord didn't seem to notice and simply stepped back, motioning with one hand that she should enter the house and saying, "Come on in."

"Thanks," Mayvee managed.

She was encouraged by the way Kord's gaze traveled over her—the fact that his smile broadened as it did. "You look so nice," he complimented. "Not that you didn't look nice last night," he politely countered. "But you look a different nice today."

"Thank you," Mayvee said, a little nervous giggle escaping her throat as she stepped into the house.

In truth, she was glad she'd had time to go home and freshen up a bit after finishing the Swansons' tree. It seemed the extra primping she'd done had paid off—assuming that his compliment was sincere, that was.

Kord couldn't help but study Mayvee Ashton from head to toe once more as she stepped over the threshold and into his grandparents' house. He'd thought she was uniquely pretty the night before at the Christmas tree lot, dressed in her work boots, worn jeans, and long knitted stocking cap over pigtails. But as cute as she'd been in her Christmas tree lot duds, the black, white, and gray striped sweater and burgundy crocheted muffler she was wearing now perfectly complemented her loose, blonde hair—long, soft blonde hair that made him want to reach out and run his fingers through it to see if it felt as nice as it looked. Kord admired how Mayvee's hair softened her appearance to the point that he half expected to look up and see some radiant beam from heaven washing over her.

The jeans she was wearing now certainly showed off her figure better than her worn ones had the night before, and when she flashed her bright, beautiful smile at him, Kord had the sudden urge to whisk her away to an afternoon of sledding, for some reason. Probably because Mayvee Ashton just looked like she'd be a lot of fun to sled with—to do anything with, actually.

The moment Mayvee stepped into the house, she was awash with a feeling of intense nostalgia—touched with a hint of melancholy. Kord's grandparents' house smelled just the way her own grandparents' houses had. Mayvee's olfactory senses were instantly alive with familiar scents—warm bread, fresh-baked cookies, and the lingering aroma of bacon. The sense of a humidifier running somewhere nearby and the ever-so-slight bouquet of Mentholatum was familiar, as well—but only barely. The heady scent of fresh pine, peppermint, and good old-fashioned home cooking were other beloved perfumes that permeated the house. All at once, Mayvee felt as if she'd walked into a home she'd been in a hundred times, instead of a house she'd never stepped foot in before.

"Oh, it smells so good in here!" she exclaimed in a breathy sigh.

"It does, doesn't it?" Kord more agreed than inquired. "It's one of the reasons I usually find myself too lazy and relaxed to leave once I've arrived." He smiled at her again, adding, "I have visions of Grandma pumping some weird sort of aromatherapy gas through the heater vents to lull me into staying longer, you know?"

Mayvee nodded and giggled. "Yeah, it smells just like my grandparents' houses used to—all warm and cozy and like you'd never have the chance to even get hungry with so much good food in the house."

"Exactly," Kord agreed. He nodded toward a well-lit room to one side of the entryway and said, "Well, come on in. I've got the lights on the tree already, and Grandma and Grandpa are nestled in on the sofa."

Mayvee's smile faded as her eyes widened with surprise. "Do…do you mean they're going to watch me decorate the tree?"

Kord chuckled. "Of course," he answered matter-of-factly—though his expression was that of understanding her discomfort. "You don't think Grandma's going to let her Ranko or Radcliff or whatever ornaments out of her sight, do you?"

"Well…well, I-I was kind of hoping she would," Mayvee stammered. "Having her watch me might make me so nervous that I might break something."

Kord's smile broadened as he said, "Oh, she wouldn't care so much. And she's not going to micromanage you. I think she and Grandpa just want to talk your ear off while you work."

"Oh," Mayvee sighed, somewhat relieved. "Well, that I can handle. I love talking with older people," she explained. "They know so much and have seen and experienced so much, you know?"

Kord nodded, agreeing, "I do know." Again he motioned toward the room to one side of the entry, and after inhaling a deep breath of determination and guts, Mayvee preceded him into it.

"Mayvee Ashton," Kord began, "these are my grandparents, George and Martha Derringer."

"Hello," Mayvee greeted the elderly couple sitting on the couch. "It's so nice to meet you."

"And you, Mayvee," George Derringer greeted as he stood and offered a hand to Mayvee. Mayvee accepted his handshake, and George chuckled, "And yes, our names really are George and Martha."

"Well, I didn't doubt it for a minute," Mayvee said, "though I do admit my ears perked up a bit when I heard it."

"I'm Martha," Kord's grandmother greeted from her seat. "I'd get up to welcome you, honey, but I've been on my knee a bit too long already today."

"Oh yes," Mayvee said. "Kord told me about your surgery. Are you recovering well?"

The white-haired woman nodded, her green eyes twinkling with the excitement of meeting someone new. "Yes, thank you. I am," she confirmed. She sighed, however, adding, "Though George and Kord—and, well, my doctor too—finally convinced me that I'm not up to decorating my own tree this year." She smiled, adding, "And so I'm very glad Kord bumped into you yesterday."

"So am I," Mayvee said. And she meant it. She glanced up into his handsome face, thinking how gorgeous he was and that meeting him was so dreamy— even if he hadn't decided to hire her to decorate his grandparent's tree. "I-I mean, I love decorating Christmas trees," she stammered, hoping that she hadn't been too obvious in her pleasure at having met Kord. "I just love seeing what kinds of ornaments people prefer, seeing what type they've added to their collections over the years and things. In fact, I hear you like Radko ornaments, Mrs. Derringer."

"Oh yes!" Martha exclaimed, clapping her hands together with excitement. "I *love* my Radko ornaments! They just reflect the lights so brilliantly, you know?"

"I do," Mayvee assured her.

She set her bag of supplies down next to the sofa, prompting George to ask, "What have you got in the bag there, sugar?"

Mayvee smiled, remembering the way her maternal grandpa used to call her sugar. She so sorely missed all of her grandparents in that moment, and her heart warmed to think that Kord still had at least one set to dote over.

"Oh, just odds and ends that I like to have on hand," she answered. "Extra hooks, ornament spinners…things like that."

"Ornament spinners?" Martha asked. "Ooo! That sounds intriguing!"

"Very," Kord added.

Mayvee looked up at him to see him smiling at her. Still, she wasn't sure whether he was teasing or in earnest in agreeing with his grandmother.

"Oh, they are intriguing," Mayvee assured her. "Especially with ornaments like Radkos. I think you'll like having a few on your tree."

"Well, I've got the lights on," Kord began. He winked at her, adding, "Per your instructions." He looked to his grandma and said, "And Grandma's. A billion and a half colored mini-lights, strung along every branch and tucked way inside to the trunk too."

Mayvee giggled with delight as Kord leaned over and plugged in an extension chord. The noble fir Kord had purchased the night before lit up so beautifully that Martha gasped with surprise and joy.

Mayvee bit her lower lip to try and contain her own delight, for it truly was a splendiferous sight to behold.

"Well, well, well, Mr. Derringer," she began, glancing up to Kord with admiration. "I can honestly say that I've never, ever, ever arrived at a home to decorate a tree to find the lights so perfectly strung!"

Kord smiled with pride, folded his muscular arms across his broad chest, and said, "Thank you. I'm pretty proud of the way it turned out."

"And it only took him two and a half hours," George added with a teasing wink and a chuckle.

Kord frowned and scolded, "Grammpa! I had her all impressed, and then you had to go and blow my cover? Sheesh!"

Mayvee laughed, and Martha winked at her.

"So? Where do we begin?" Kord inquired then.

"Well, I usually start with the specialty ornaments," Mayvee began to explain. "You know, shaped ones or family heirlooms." She looked to Martha and said, "Your Radkos—that would be where I'd like to start."

"Oh, of course!" Martha exclaimed. "That's where I always start too. I had Kord get them out of storage with the rest of the tree stuff. Where did you put the Radkos, Kord honey?"

"Right here," Kord answered.

Mayvee watched him stride to the other side of the room and retrieve a large plastic bin. He picked it up and carried it over to Mayvee. "Where do you want it?" he asked.

"Oh, just right to one side of the tree please," she said. She looked to Martha and said, "I can't wait to see your ornaments, Mrs. Derringer! You have to promise to tell me if any of them have special stories, okay?"

"Oh, of course, Mayvee! I'd love to!" Martha chirped.

Kord exhaled a sigh of relief. In truth, his grandmother hadn't been too keen on the idea of allowing someone else to decorate her Christmas tree—especially a stranger. But Kord had known the minute he'd seen Mayvee talking with an elderly man at the tree lot the night before that she would have a way with his grandparents—especially his grandmother. He was glad he'd been right—he was glad he'd hired her—he was glad he got to watch her decorate a Christmas tree. She was so cute, pretty, and beautiful all at the same time that he figured he'd enjoy watching her do anything.

Taking a seat in one of the armchairs across from the sofa where his grandparents sat, Kord stretched, yawned a little, and tucked his hands behind his head. He was settled in for the remainder of the afternoon—settled in and ready to watch the tree lot girl work her magic.

And watch her he did—for almost three hours! For nearly three hours Kord was more than happy to sit in his grandma's armchair and listen to the conversation between Mayvee and his grandmother. He was amazed, not only at how well Mayvee related with his grandmother but also by what he learned about Mayvee.

As Mayvee decorated his grandparents' Christmas tree, Kord learned that her father was in the military—on his final deployment before retiring. He learned that Mayvee's parents had inherited the Christmas tree lot, outbuildings, and fields from Mayvee's father's parents. Mayvee had two siblings, an older brother and a younger one, both of whom Kord had met at the tree lot. He learned that Mayvee's previous boyfriend had encouraged her to get her real estate agent's license and that she had and that she had likewise learned that the real estate business was not for her. She'd been looking for something that she could work around college classes but was now certain that it would never again be real estate. Mayvee assured Kord's grandmother that, although she loved the Christmas tree lot and selling Christmas trees, it was because she loved matching people to the tree that was just right for them—and although real estate involved matching properties to people, it wasn't anything the same otherwise to Mayvee.

The other thing that amazed Kord was the way she changed a simple fir tree into a work of art! His grandmother's tree stood in the bay window beckoning onlookers inside and out like a bright, shining beacon of beauty. Oh sure, Kord had seen a lot of Christmas trees in his lifetime, but nothing that made him feel as warm and rather sentimental as his grandma and grandpa's tree did in that moment that Mayvee put the last strands of silver icicles on it.

"The trick is to put several strands together, and only on the tips of some branches," Mayvee said to Martha as she stepped back to study the tree. "That way you still get the reflective properties of the icicles without hiding all your beautiful ornaments, Mrs. Derringer."

Martha put her hands to her mouth a moment, shaking her head in awe. Mayvee tried not to feel too proud about how beautiful the tree had turned out—for the ornaments were already Mrs. Derringer's choices and collection—but she couldn't help but feel a little bit giddy, for it was certainly a beautiful tree.

"Oh, Mayvee!" Martha exclaimed. "It's so beautiful. It's just perfect and so beautiful!"

Mayvee sighed with relief and satisfaction as she saw the moisture of still growing wonderment in Martha's eyes. Mayvee loved to make people happy, and she could see that Martha Derringer was happy in that moment.

"Are you finished then?" Mr. Derringer asked.

"Oh yes. And I'm so sorry it took so long, Mr. Derringer," Mayvee began. "But I don't like to rush. I just want everything to come together as well as it can."

"I'm not rushing you, sugar," Mr. Derringer assured her. "It's just…now it's time for my favorite part."

Mayvee giggled. "And what's that?" she asked.

"Breakfast for supper!" Mr. Derringer and Kord exclaimed in unison.

Mayvee looked to Martha, puzzled, as Kord and his grandpa fairly hopped up from their seats and headed for the kitchen.

Martha laughed. "It's a family tradition," she explained. "After we decorate the tree, we have breakfast for supper—pancakes or French toast or waffles, hashbrowns, bacon, and orange juice."

"Oh, sounds delicious!" Mayvee giggled. "Well, I'll just be on my way and—"

"Oh, but surely you'll stay for supper, won't you?" Martha asked. Mayvee could see by the pleading in the old woman's eyes that she was sincere in her invitation.

"Well, I wouldn't want to impose, Mrs. Derringer," Mayvee stammered. "It's a family tradition and—"

"I'll pay you," Kord said, stepping back into the living room. "You can charge me for the time, if you like. But you can't leave without the traditional breakfast for supper—especially after that work of art in the bay window. I mean, ornament spinners? Who knew?"

He smiled, winked at Mayvee, and stepped back into the kitchen. "You won't have to do anything, by the way," he called. "Grandpa and I made the pancake batter earlier, and the bacon won't take long. So don't think you're getting away, tree lot girl."

Martha smiled, reached out, and took Mayvee's hand. Her hand was warm and soft, and Mayvee could feel the dear wrinkles of age stretched over the tired bones of her fingers.

"Please stay, Mayvee," Martha pleaded.

Mayvee felt tears begin to well in her eyes. Her heart had always been so tender when it came to the elderly. And anyway, how could she say no to a woman whose grandson was more handsome than any movie actor to have ever walked the earth?

"All right," she agreed, at last. "If you're sure it's not an imposition."

Martha's eyes lit up with a sparkle that revealed her joy. "Not at all, honey. We're delighted to have you." Martha winked at Mayvee and giggled. "Possibly one of us even more than others."

Mayvee blushed and shook her head with awkwardness. Still, she couldn't help but wonder how fabulous it would be if Mrs. Derringer's implication were factual.

CHAPTER THREE

"So how much did all this set you back, Kord?" George asked his grandson as Kord returned from seeing Mayvee to her car.

"What? Do you mean having your tree decorated for you guys?" Kord asked, rubbing his hands together to warm them.

"Yes," George confirmed. "Seems like that would be a pretty expensive service, especially with the way your grandma talked the poor girl's head off." Kord smiled as his grandpa chuckled, adding, "Not to mention the way we roped her into staying for supper with us."

"Yeah, I suppose we might have taken up too much of her time," Kord admitted. But as his smile broadened, he said, "But I'm glad we did."

George laughed again and winked at his grandson with understanding as he said, "I'm sure you are."

Kord laughed a bit too then. His grandpa might be a lot older than he once was, but he still knew how to spot a fine young woman.

"So? Are you gonna toss your hat in the ring here, boy?" Kord's grandpa asked.

Kord shrugged. "I'd like to…but she's a pretty sweet thing. I'm sure she's got every guy she knows running after her with his tongue hanging out."

"Well, you won't know unless you try," his grandpa pointed out. "But the way you were sitting in that chair all afternoon, watching that girl decorate the tree and wearing a goofy grin, I'd say you definitely should go fishing for her."

"What goofy grin?" Kord asked, feigning ignorance.

"The one that tells me and your grandpa that girl has already begun to wrap you around her finger, Kord," his grandma called from the kitchen. "And you still didn't answer your grandpa's question about how much this whole evening set you back!"

Kord and George both smiled, shaking their heads with amusement.

"The woman has ears like a bat," George whispered.

"I heard that, George!" Martha called again.

George rolled his eyes, and Kord chuckled.

"Well, do you have a plan yet?" George asked.

"For what?" Kord asked, again feigning ignorance.

"For throwing your hat in the ring for that Mayvee girl," George reminded with teasing exasperation.

But Kord shook his head, amused at his grandpa's overzealous encouragement. "Grandpa, you do know that I had only seen her once before today, don't you?"

George's smile broadened as he nodded in return, saying, "Well, there was a time when I had only seen your grandma once before, now wasn't there?"

"She did a *beautiful* job decorating our Christmas tree," Kord's grandmother again called from the kitchen. "And I already like her better than any other girl you've ever brought over for us to meet."

"I didn't bring her over just to meet you, Grandma," Kord called. "I hired her to decorate your Christmas tree, remember?"

"Oh, quit hollering at me and just come on in here, honey," his grandma laughed. "Besides, someone needs to finish up this leftover bacon, and my knee is sore right now so I'd like to keep my seat in here."

Kord's grandpa patted him on the back as they headed toward the kitchen. "So how much did hiring that cute little tree decorator of yours set you back anyway?"

♥

Kord turned the key in his truck's ignition and shivered against the cold. He reached forward, turning up the heater as his teeth began to chatter. His grandma was right: he should've worn a coat.

As he shifted into first, Kord smiled—pleased with himself for having managed to skirt answering his grandparents' questions about how much he'd paid Mayvee to decorate the tree. After all, it was part of his Christmas gift to his grandparents, so they didn't need to know. Furthermore, he couldn't think of anything in all the world worth more than the opportunity to watch Mayvee Ashton decorate his grandma's Christmas tree. The fact that she'd been so kind and conversational with his grandparents (even stayed for dinner when they'd insisted) was a bonus he'd never expected.

As he pulled away from the curb in front of his grandparents' house, he glanced over for one more look at the beautiful Christmas tree beaming in their front bay window. In that very instant, it was like a truckload of Christmas lights lit up in his head. Why not toss his hat in the ring, as his grandpa had put it? Kord hadn't denied for one minute the fact that he'd been instantly attracted to Mayvee the night before at the Christmas tree lot—really attracted to her, sort of magnetically so. This attraction was different; it went far beyond the mere physical, for, from the moment he saw her, he found that he'd wanted to know everything about her. He'd even felt a sense of already knowing some things about her, even though they'd never met before. It was weird—and he couldn't explain it.

He'd spent three hours watching Mayvee Ashton decorate his grandma's tree and one hour with her at a pancake supper, and the way he'd felt pretty much let down once he'd seen her to her car and watched her drive away afterward. One thing he did know: a woman had never so completely captured his attention and interest before. She was beautiful and kind, had a good sense of humor, and was just plain incredible to be around. So he'd throw his hat in the ring and see what happened.

Kord chuckled to himself, realizing that he'd already formulated a plan in his head to see Mayvee again, even before she'd arrived at his grandparents' house that afternoon. If that weren't a sign of his subconscious telling him to go for it, his grandpa and grandma's encouragement to do so was.

"A guy can't ignore signs like that, right?" he asked himself aloud. He switched on the satellite radio, leaned back into his seat, and let his determination to pursue Mayvee Ashton gather momentum as he drove the rest of the way home.

♥

Plopping down on the sofa in the front room, Mayvee sighed with both fatigue and satisfaction. She'd worked at the tree lot all morning, decorated Mr. and Mrs. Swanson's Christmas tree, decorated Mr. and Mrs. Derringer's tree, enjoyed a delicious supper with Kord and his grandparents, and then worked the tree lot until midnight. She was tired! Still, it was the good kind of tired—the tired one felt from a hard day's work doing something one liked to do. Therefore, Mayvee was content, relishing the warm fire in the fireplace and the mug of hot cocoa her mother had made for her.

"So?" Craig said as he rather collapsed into the chair next to the sofa.

"So what?" Mayvee asked. Oh sure, she knew what Craig was "so-ing" about, but she'd decided to play ignorant anyway.

"So? How was your date with Dagwood today?" Craig asked.

Mayvee rolled her eyes with amused exasperation. "I didn't have a date today, and I certainly don't know anyone named Dagwood."

"Oh, come on," Craig prodded. He took a sip of his own hot chocolate. "How was he? You know,

Dagwood? Did you decorate his tree well enough to suit him?"

"His name is Kord, and it wasn't his tree, and stop being stupid," Mayvee answered. "And yes, I do believe his grandparents were pleased with the way their tree turned out. After all, they insisted I stay for supper with them—pancakes and bacon!"

"Oooo! Already won over the grandparents, did you? You work fast," Craig teased.

"I wish," Mayvee sighed.

Craig's brows arched with mild astonishment. "You do? You mean, the sparks I saw flying out of your ears when Dagwood said his first words to you weren't my imagination?"

Mayvee stared at her brother with obvious sarcasm in her expression. "Craig, did you see Kord Derringer? Did you see his broad shoulders, his dark hair, beautiful eyes, perfectly square chin, straight nose, dark eyelashes, perfect lips, long legs—"

"I noticed he was a dude and that your ears were spitting sparks," Craig interrupted.

Mayvee rolled her eyes again. "Oh, come on, Craig. He's so gorgeous, and you know it."

"Well, if you say so," Craig mumbled. "He had a nice truck, so I guess that's something."

"Oh, brother," Mayvee mumbled. "Of course my ears were spitting sparks when I saw him, you dork! He's beautiful!"

Craig shook his head. "If any woman ever calls me beautiful, just put me out of my misery."

"Don't worry, man," Josh said, striding into the room with his own mug of steamy hot cocoa. "There's no danger of that ever happening." He laughed to indicate he was teasing, slapped his big brother on one shoulder, and sat down in front of the fireplace.

"What? You or Mayvee putting me out of my misery?" Craig laughed.

"Of a woman ever calling you beautiful," Josh chuckled.

"Shut up," Craig mumbled into his mug.

"Hey, Mayvee," Josh began, "can you poop the trees tomorrow for about an hour while I run up to the mall and pick up Mom's Christmas gift?"

"Probably," Mayvee said. "Just try to go during a lull in customers, okay?"

"I will," Josh said. He exhaled a tired sigh and drank some cocoa. After a moment, he asked, "Do you guys feel okay about leaving Mom and Aunt Sondra at the tree lot tonight? I mean, it's just kind of weird to think of them as the property guards, you know?"

Mayvee and Craig exchanged understanding glances as Craig answered, "They'll be okay, Josh. They've got food and heat and a TV and movies to watch."

"No, I mean…do you think they'll be safe?" Josh asked.

Mayvee understood how Josh was feeling. Every year before, her father had always stayed overnight at the tree lot during the Christmas tree selling season. In fact, every year Mayvee looked forward to the one or two nights a week that it was her turn to stay with her father to "guard" the lot.

The small room in the very back of the sales center was a cozy, dreamy sort of place. Warmed by a small space heater and complete with a tiny fridge filled with water, sodas, and snacks, the tree lot "hideaway" (as her father always called it) was a magical place to everyone in the Ashton family. Mayvee had so many fond memories of sitting on the bed all cuddled up in her dad's strong arms watching Christmas specials or Christmas movies on the small TV that sat on a table at the foot of it. Her mother had strung mini Christmas lights here and there over the ceiling, and Mayvee would drift to sleep gazing up at them, imagining they were tiny, twinkling, colored stars.

Her brothers both took turns staying with her father on certain nights too—and her mother even had her sister, Sondra, come and stay at the house with Mayvee, Craig, and Josh while she spent a few nights away, tucked in at the tree lot hideaway with her husband.

And yet now that her father was so far away, and in constant danger, Mayvee didn't feel as safe at the tree lot at night, and she understood Josh's concerns about their mother's safety as well.

So wanting to soothe her own worries as well as those of her little brother, she said, "Well, first of all, they're both packing heat, and they're better shots than most men."

"And second, they'll probably stay up all night playing cards or talking about old boyfriends and never go to sleep at all," Craig added. "They'll be fine, Josh."

Mayvee smiled, however, for she knew Craig had taken his phone out of his pocket in that moment with the intent of texting their mom and making sure all was well.

"Well, okay," Josh sighed. "If you guys say so…I guess I'll try not to worry."

"Now, where were we?" Craig asked, shoving his phone back in his pocket.

"You were grilling Mayvee about the dude that she was drooling over yesterday," Josh offered.

"I was not drooling over him," Mayvee mildly defended herself. "But I will say this. He can flip my pancakes anytime."

Josh and Craig exchanged perplexed glances.

"Is that like a euphemism or something?" Josh asked.

"More like a metaphor, I think…because she stayed at his grandparents' house for dinner after she finished their tree," Craig explained. "They had pancakes."

"Oh, sweet," Josh said. He looked to Mayvee. "So? Did he ask you out?"

"No," Mayvee admitted, feeling defeated, depressed, and sort of angry all at once.

"Well, did you ask him out?" Craig asked.

"Heck no!" Mayvee exclaimed. "What kind of a girl do you think I am?"

Craig shook his head. "Well, how do you ever expect to see him again?"

"Maybe you could decorate his personal Christmas tree," Josh suggested. "No metaphor intended." He and Craig both snickered into their mugs.

"He didn't say anything about having one," Mayvee said. "And besides, what was I supposed to do? Say, 'Hey, handsome, do you have any other trees that need decorating? I'd love to do them for you!' He'd think I was whacked out!"

"Well, I know if a pretty girl offered to decorate my tree for me," Craig began, trying not to laugh, "I'd sure as hell let her!"

Josh and Craig both burst into laughter then, amused at their own naughty insinuations.

But Mayvee shook her head with mild—though not admitted—amusement, got up from her place on the sofa, and said, "You guys are such dorks. I'm going to bed."

"Oh, don't be mad, Mayvee," Craig called after her. "We're just teasing you."

"I know," she said. "But you're still dorks."

She smiled as she heard her brothers laughing and quietly making up more metaphors.

"I think that dude really sizzled Mayvee's bacon," she heard Josh laugh.

"Really melted her butter!" she heard Craig counter.

Still smiling over her brothers' ridiculousness as she entered her bedroom and closed the door behind her, Mayvee was upset with herself for not having thought of a way to see Kord again. It wasn't like she'd never seen or met a good-looking guy at the tree lot over the years—but Kord was different. There was something so...so unique about him—about the way he made her feel when he looked at her, like fireworks really were shooting from her ears and her arms and legs had turned to hot jelly.

Of course, Mayvee figured Kord made every girl feel that way when he looked at her. She was sure she wasn't anything special in that regard. But it was more than that—like the way he treated his grandparents and the fact that he stayed with them the whole time she was decorating their tree, had dinner with them afterward, and tried to pay her extra for staying for dinner with them. He just seemed to be a throwback kind of man—like he should be wearing jeans, workboots, and a flannel shirt and carrying an ax—and then suddenly disappear into a wardrobe room and come out wearing a tuxedo and carrying a Walther and introducing himself as, "Derringer, Kord Derringer."

"But wait!" Mayvee whispered aloud to herself as she went into her bathroom to brush her teeth. "Jeans, boots, no shirt, and a cowboy hat!" She giggled as she squeezed the toothpaste tube, putting toothpaste on her toothbrush. "Yeah, yeah! That's it!" she giggled as she brushed. "He could *so* pull that off!"

Yet when Mayvee climbed into bed a few minutes later, it was with a heavy, heavy burden of regret weighing on her mind—and her heart. She felt like something weighty had been laid on her chest, as if she'd missed the opportunity of a lifetime by not finding a way to see Kord again before she'd left him at his grandparents' house.

"Well, what do you have to offer anyway, Mayvee?" she asked herself as she tried to push images of the handsome, blue-green-eyed near-stranger from her mind—as she tried not to worry about her mother and her Aunt Sondra keeping watch over the Christmas tree lot through the night.

"You still live at home, you're between jobs…and you're too chicken to have asked him to lunch or something before you left," she mumbled.

Still, a tiny flicker of hope did twinkle in her chest as she drifted off to sleep. After all, she had his contact information on the form he'd filled out when he'd hired her to decorate his grandparents' tree. Maybe she could think of a reason to call him. Maybe she could take a little "thank you for your business" gift to his grandparents and happen upon Kord visiting them. Either way, the tiny twinkle of hope was enough to allow Mayvee to drift off to sleep—and with visions of Kord Derringer dressed as a cowboy dancing in her dreams.

CHAPTER FOUR

"Well, no wonder they're tired," Craig said as he and Mayvee stood watching their mother and Aunt Sondra driving away from the tree lot. "Mom said they stayed up all night watching chick flicks."

Mayvee smiled as she thought of her mother and aunt tucked into the tiny back room of the sales center, eating Goobers and Raisinets, and watching movies. It seemed her mom never took any time to just relax. So even though Mayvee knew her mom and Aunt Sondra were staying at the tree lot to keep an eye on things, she was glad they'd had so much fun.

"I'm on guard duty tonight, and I'll say this: I'm sleeping!" Craig stated with determination.

"So you're admitting to me that you plan on sleeping on the job?" Mayvee teased.

"Heck yeah!" Craig said, frowning to indicate how serious he was. "I have to work tomorrow, so I can't stay up too late anyway." He paused, rubbed his hands together to warm them, and said, "I think I'll go ahead and build a fire in the fire pit. The customers always enjoy it, plus it's handy when my hands and butt get cold."

Mayvee shook her head and playfully scolded, "I swear, Craig, you can take the romance out of anything!"

Craig quirked an eyebrow. "I work here, Mayvee. I don't have the luxury of standing around the fire pit sipping cocoa with some hot girl next to me."

Mayvee rolled her eyes with exasperation. "You miss the whole point of the fire pit, you ding-dong. It creates an atmosphere of winter and warmth. The smell of wood burning soothes people and makes them happy."

Craig nodded. "Yeah. So they'll buy a Christmas tree."

Mayvee sighed with mild disgust. "Forget it. You're such a man."

But Craig's attention was suddenly arrested by something behind and beyond Mayvee. "Hey," he began, "isn't that Dagwood's truck? Yeah, it is! I never forget a pickup. He's back—your dream man!"

"What?" Mayvee gasped, spinning around just in time to see Kord Derringer getting out of his black pickup. "It *is* him!" she whispered, astonished.

Craig chuckled. "Wow! He really must've liked the way you decorated his tree! He's back for seconds."

"Shut up," Mayvee grumbled. "And don't start."

Craig laughed. "I guess you'll be wanting to wait on this customer, huh?"

"Yes," she said flatly. Glancing back up at him, she added, "Why don't you go help Josh poop a tree or something?"

"You mean, make like a tree and leaf," Craig stated, still smiling with amusement.

"Yes…and sooner than later," Mayvee added. "He's coming right this way."

But Craig disobeyed and lingered until Kord walked right up to them.

"How's it going…Dagwood, is it?" Craig asked, offering a hand to Kord.

"Kord, actually," Kord said, shaking Craig's hand.

"Well, I hope you don't mind if I let Mayvee help you out, Kord," Craig said. "I've got to get a fire going in the fire pit—you know, to add a romantic atmosphere to the tree lot."

"Sure," Kord said. "I…uh…I was hoping to talk to Mayvee anyway." He looked to Mayvee, grinning and causing goose bumps to ripple over her arms.

"Oh?" Craig asked.

"Yeah. I was wondering if she had any time to decorate another tree for me…at my office," Kord explained.

"Well, I'm sure she does," Craig answered. Mayvee blushed as she felt him poke her in the back with his index finger to indicate he understood she was delighted Kord had another decorating job for her. "I'll just let you two get to it then. Good to see you again, Kord."

"You too," Kord said with a nod.

Craig strode away, leaving Mayvee alone with Kord. She found she was rather tongue-tied, because he didn't say anything at first—just stood before her grinning as he looked down at her.

"Do...do your grandparents still like their tree?" she began. "They're not having someone-decorated-our-tree-for-us remorse, are they?"

Kord's smile broadened. "No, not at all." He paused, frowned a little, and then asked, "*Is* there such a thing?"

Mayvee smiled and shrugged. "I don't really know. But I certainly hope not."

Kord chuckled. The low, pleasing intonation of his amusement sent goose bumps racing over Mayvee's arms again.

"My grandma and grandpa love their tree," he reassured her. "And I got to thinking...it sure was easy to let someone else do it for them, you know? Instead of me having to do it by myself."

"Yeah?" Mayvee encouraged. She would love to decorate another tree for Kord! Maybe he would even be lingering around his office when she was there, and that would give her the opportunity to not only stare at his manly gorgeousness but also get to know him better. Maybe.

"I usually put a tree up in the front office of my business, or I have one of my employees do it. But my receptionist had to quit because she has a new baby, and I just don't feel like I have the time to do it myself. I'm feeling really swamped and short-handed, you know?"

"I'm sure," Mayvee agreed—though she had no idea what Kord's business even was. "Um...what kind of business are you in anyway? If you don't mind my asking."

He smiled. "Not at all. I make acrylic aquariums. I do a lot of custom work but also provide basic aquariums and maintenance services and things," he explained.

"Oh!" Mayvee exclaimed. "Like the guys on the Animal Planet series. I *love* that show!"

"Yeah, me too," he said as his dazzling smile broadened. "Those guys are intense. I've seen some of their custom aquariums. They're unreal." He shrugged. "But me, I'm just a regular guy, without a cable show. I do custom jobs, but I also have store that sells everything a person needs to set up a basic aquarium—from a little bowl and a betta fish to bigger ones. And I provide a home service to people who don't want to deal with maintaining their tanks but love aquariums and fish habitats. It pays the bills, and it's something I enjoy doing."

"So you like fish," Mayvee stated. Instantly she realized how ridiculous her statement sounded, but it was already out of her mouth, so there was nothing she could do about it.

Again he laughed. "Yeah, I do," he confirmed. "And you must like decorating Christmas trees."

"Yeah, I do," she giggled, delighted by Kord's easy manner in teasing her.

"So? How would you like to decorate mine?" he asked.

Mayvee thought about the ridiculous teasing her brothers had given her the night before and bit her lip to keep from giggling.

She managed to answer, "I would love to! When would you like to have it decorated?"

"How about Tuesday late afternoon...*if* your decorating schedule is open?" Kord asked. He grinned and asked, "And can I treat you to dinner when you're finished?"

Mayvee felt her eyes widen in astonishment. She certainly hadn't expected Kord to ask her to dinner! Finally able to draw a breath, she found she was stunned into silence for a moment—but only a moment.

"Sure!" she managed, at last. She knew she sounded way too excited about the prospect of having dinner with Kord—again—and without his sweet grandparents. But she didn't care. She'd worry about appearing too eager later.

"Great," Kord said, his incredible smile broadening. "And why don't you just let me pick you up and bring you to my office to do the tree? Then we can go straight to dinner. I'll take you home afterward, of course."

"That would be perfect," Mayvee assured him. She couldn't stop smiling up at him! She knew she probably looked like a lovesick puppy, but she couldn't reel herself in.

"Okay then," Kord said, nodding. "What time should I pick you up for an exciting afternoon of Christmas tree decorating Tuesday?" he asked. "And where?"

"Um, about four, and I'll be working here before that. So just pick me up here, I guess," she answered. "If that's not too much trouble."

"Nope. Not at all," he confirmed. "So I guess I'll see you Tuesday at four then."

"Yeah," Mayvee said—*still* smiling at him like a lovesick puppy. "Oh!" she said, finally managing to consciously think about the job to do for him before dinner. "Is your tree pre-lit? Or does it need to have lights put on?" she asked. "I'm assuming it's an artificial tree, since most businesses don't use fresh-cut trees because of fire and insurance reasons and stuff."

Kord smiled, trying not to reveal the fact that he hadn't even thought of lights on the tree. The fact was he didn't even own a tree for his front office. He'd just borrowed one of his mom's old artificial ones on previous years, and that old tree would never do now.

But Kord was nothing if not quick on his feet, so he answered, "Yep, you guessed it. Artificial and pre-lit."

"Great!" she said. "And you have all your own ornaments and stuff, right?"

Again Kord nodded. "Yep," he answered—simultaneously thinking that he'd better remember to pick up some ornaments too, when he stopped to pick up a new pre-lit tree.

"Excuse me, miss," a thirty-something-aged woman interrupted. "Do you work here?"

Mayvee was irritated—not only because the customer had interrupted her conversation with Kord but also because she stood smiling at him and batting her eyes like a fool.

"Yes, I do," Mayvee answered politely, however. "I'll be right with you, ma'am."

"Okay," the woman said, still grinning at Kord—still looking him up and down like he were some giant, decadent dessert.

"I'll let you get back to work," Kord said.

Although Mayvee's heart sunk to the pit of her stomach with a thud of disappointment, she sighed, "I guess so," with agreement.

"Tomorrow at four then," he confirmed.

"On this very spot," she assured him.

"Great! Have a good day, Mayvee," Kord said. He smiled at her once more and then turned to leave.

"You too, Kord," she called after him. He turned and tossed a nod to her before striding away toward his truck.

She exhaled a heavy sigh of admiration as she watched his manly walk for a moment longer. Turning to the waiting customer, Mayvee asked, "How may I help you?"

♥

Kord's office was downtown, just a few miles from his grandparents' home. As he parked his truck in front of a parking meter a few yards from his business, Mayvee wondered where Kord actually lived. Did he live on his own—nearby? Did he have a roommate? Did he still live at home the way she did to save money for tuition?

There was so much she didn't know about him. Yet as Mayvee sat in his truck waiting for him to come around to the passenger's side and open the door for her the way he'd asked her to, she didn't care so much. Each of the three times she'd seen him, she'd learned more and more about him. Decorating his office space Christmas tree would be another chance to get to know him better. And then—then there would be dinner with him afterward! She had enjoyed having breakfast for supper with Kord and his grandparents so much that she couldn't begin to imagine how wonderful enjoying a meal with him alone would be.

"Here we are," Kord said, opening the passenger's side door of his truck. "The good old Bailey Building and Loan."

Mayvee laughed, delighted at his random reference to one of her favorite movies of all time, *It's a Wonderful Life*.

"You've been given a great gift, George: a chance to see what the world would be like without you," Mayvee quoted in return.

Kord's smile broadened with admiration, and he nodded. "Well, well, well. Have I found a fellow appreciator of classic movies?"

"Yes," Mayvee answered, delighted that she'd pleased him. "Well, classic Christmas movies, at least."

"I'll take it," Kord chuckled. He nodded toward a storefront with an eye-catching sign that read *Somethin' Fishy* above the front entrance. "I think I've got everything together for you."

As Kord opened the door to his store, allowing Mayvee to precede him in entering, she was instantly struck by the lack of fish smell in the front office. In fact, she had so expected Somethin' Fishy to smell...well, fishy, that she actual said aloud, "Hmm. It smells good in here."

Kord laughed. "You sound so surprised," he said.

Blushing, Mayvee admitted, "Well, I did kind of think it might smell like the seafood section of the grocery store, you know?"

"Yeah, I think a lot of people expect that," he said. "But sometimes if you wait a second or two, and if the smell of the acrylic happens to waft up here, you might start wishing that it did smell more like grocery store fish."

Mayvee looked at him, knowing her smile was as broad as it could possibly be. He was so handsome, so clever, so nice—so built!

Kord couldn't keep from smiling as he studied Mayvee a moment. She was so pretty—so soft and alluring in her pink sweater and cute little jeans and boots. Her long blonde hair hung over her shoulders looking like silk and seeming to capture any light that was nearby and hold it as its own.

He was struck as he realized that one of the many reasons he was drawn to her was her complete femininity. She worked moving Christmas trees—netting them and tying them to the tops of people's cars—proof that she was strong and tough and willing to do hard work. And yet she still managed to stay completely a girl—a woman.

From the time he was a kid, Kord had been disturbed by the seeming lack of feminine women. It just appeared to him that the majority of women in the world were so into themselves and competing with men that they'd toughened up too much—lost the soft, nurturing nature he associated with a desirable woman. Oh, he firmly believed that women should get paid what men got paid for doing the same job, and he didn't believe that women were lesser to a man's mind. In fact, it was his firm opinion that most good women were wiser, emotionally stronger, and less likely to falter than most men—even good men. As a compliment to his respect for women, Kord also felt that men should be what they were created to be—protectors, providers, heroic champions who would give life and limb in defense of their women and children.

And it was that core belief and feeling in his soul—the desire and need, the determination, to be a woman's masculine, manly hero—that was attracting him to this soft, beautiful, yet strong and fully capable Christmas tree decorator. In that moment, standing in his aquarium shop, Kord realized that Mayvee Ashton was the woman he'd been looking for—the beautiful, feminine, strong woman he wanted.

"Well, I guess I better get started," Mayvee said, blushing as Kord continued to stare at her. She wondered what in the world he was thinking about, because he looked totally zoned out—as if his mind were in some other place entirely. But she took heart in the fact that he was still smiling at her—that his beautiful blue-green eyes were glistening with…with something. Amusement maybe? She wasn't sure. But whatever it was, it was almost certainly a good thing.

"Yeah," Kord agreed, snapping out of whatever had caused him to just stand there staring at her. "The sooner you're finished, the sooner we can eat, right?"

"Right," Mayvee agreed.

MARCIA LYNN MCCLURE

"So I set up the tree, right over there, as you can see," he said, pointing to a prelit, artificial tree about eight feet high, positioned in the front window of his shop. "I just tossed the boxes of ornaments and stuff there in the corner. I'll admit, I'm pretty lame when it comes to stuff like this...so I hope you have what you need."

Mayvee smiled at him, thinking how adorable it was that he felt awkward about Christmas tree décor. "I'm sure I do. If I need anything else, I'll ask you. Or maybe I'll happen to have it in my bag here." She patted her bag of extra supplies before setting it down on the floor at her feet.

"Okay. Sounds good," Kord said. "I'll just be in the back if you need anything." He paused a moment, adding, "Like I said, I'm short-handed right now, so I might come running in here and there if the phone rings. But other than that, I'll stay out of your hair."

"Oh, you won't be in my hair," Mayvee said, thinking that she'd love nothing more than to know what it felt like to have his strong hands run through her hair. She glanced at the empty reception desk then. "So you really don't have anyone to answer calls?"

"Nope," Kord confirmed. He exhaled a heavy, discouraged sort of sigh. "And this time of year, it's rough. I've got to get on that and hire somebody." He looked at her and smiled. "You're not looking for a job by any chance, are you?"

"Not until after Christmas," Mayvee answered. "Mom and Craig have me pretty booked up at the lot until December 25."

"What about after that?" Kord asked unexpectedly. "Are you…do you…what do you usually do…when the lot isn't open, I mean?"

Mayvee sighed this time, rolled her eyes, and answered, "Well, that's a long story actually."

"Good! You can tell me at dinner," he said. The phone rang that very moment, and Kord said, "I better get that. So I'll let you get to it."

"Okay," Mayvee said, smiling at him as she watched him hurry to the phone.

Kord picked up the phone receiver and said, "This is Kord."

Mayvee watched Kord rummage around in one drawer of the desk until he found a Bluetooth. "Uh huh…yes, we can do that," he said. He winked at her, attached the Bluetooth to his ear, and headed to the back of the shop.

Instantly Mayvee was struck with a sensation of the room being colder and not as bright as it had been when Kord had been standing in it. She felt lonesome all of a sudden—and the unexpected emotion unsettled her.

So rubbing her hands together in determining that the sooner she finished decorating Kord's Christmas tree, the sooner she could be alone with him at dinner, Mayvee went over and sat on the floor in front of the boxes of ornaments. Picking up a box containing four vintage-looking glass ornaments, she was surprised to find the sides of the top of the box still taped to the bottom of the box—almost as if the box had never been opened before.

"Wow! What a fastidious guy you are, Kord Derringer," she mumbled to herself. In truth, she had a hard time imagining any guy being so careful with packing away Christmas ornaments. Once she opened the box, she found that no hooks lingered on the ornaments from the year before. She searched through the boxes of ornaments to find a package of new, never-opened, never-used, gold ornament hooks.

"What? Do you buy new hooks every year?" she giggled to herself. But as she began to open the package of ornament hooks, she noticed something else—price tags on some of the gold string attached to some of the loose ornaments.

"It's almost like…" she thought aloud to herself.

"Like I went out last night and bought all new ornaments or something?" Kord said from behind her.

Mayvee looked around to see Kord standing behind her, grinning with a rather guilty expression on his handsome face.

"Well…yeah," she admitted. "I mean, do you really buy new ornament hooks every year?"

"Nope," Kord answered. "This is the first year I've bought ornament hooks…ever."

"Oh," Mayvee said, frowning. She looked at the loose glass ornaments lying on the floor—picked up another box of ornaments to find that it looked as if it had never been opened as well. "But all your ornaments…they all look brand new."

Kord laughed, tapped the Bluetooth at his ear, and said, "This is Kord." He winked at Mayvee and whispered, "I think you'll figure it out here in a minute."

He left the room again, heading toward the back of the store.

"Figure what out?" Mayvee asked aloud. As she sat looking around for a second or two, her attention was arrested by a department store bag nearby. She could see boxes of icicles sticking out of it and decided to see what else was in the bag.

Boxes of icicles, another package of unopened ornament hooks, and several ornament spinners were in the bag—along with a receipt. Now, Mayvee had not intended to be nosy—it wasn't like her at all. But when her gaze fell to the date on the receipt, she gasped a little. The receipt was dated the day before and included multiple boxes of ornaments, individual ornaments, icicles, ornament hooks, ornament spinners—and a prelit artificial Christmas tree.

At first Mayvee thought she must be imagining the fact that the time stamp on the receipt was well after the time when Kord had stopped by the tree lot to hire her to decorate his tree. But as realization began to wash over her, so did the euphoria of understanding: Kord had hired her to decorate his office tree before he'd even had an office tree to decorate!

Mayvee shook her head and thought, "Maybe his tree was just old and all his ornaments were broken or something, and he decided this would be a good year to replace them. Yeah…that must be it."

Even still, as Mayvee busily decorated Kord's Christmas tree, she couldn't help but wonder if perhaps he'd hired her just so he could take her to dinner afterward. She was sure it wasn't true—but what was the harm in pretending that it was?

CHAPTER FIVE

Mayvee had done an incredible job decorating the tree for the store—at least Kord assumed she had. The truth was, he had barely glanced at the finished product. After all, there wasn't a Christmas tree in the world that could be more stunning, more interesting, or more attention-grabbing than Mayvee Ashton standing in front of him in her pretty pink sweater.

Even now, as he sat across the table from her at the diner, he was momentarily lost in the ethereal beauty of her green-blue eyes—mesmerized by her perfectly smooth, perfectly flawless skin and the rosy pink on her cheeks.

"So tell me what you're into," Mayvee said, drawing Kord's attention back to their conversation. She smiled, adding, "Other than building aquariums, of course."

Kord smiled and answered, "Stuff that goes in aquariums."

Mayvee's expression changed to that of amusement at his sarcasm. "I sort of figured *that* went without saying." She sipped the water from her glass and prodded, "But seriously, what else do you do with your free time? You know, for fun?" She smiled with mischief, asking, "Any special talents that you're hiding?"

Kord laughed. He knew she had at least two brothers, so he wondered whether she had really walked into asking that question without imagining all the clever, flirtatious comebacks that it had inspired in him. But being that it was their first date, he figured he better play nice.

"You mean like playing an instrument or something?" he asked.

"Yeah," Mayvee answered, sipping her water through her straw again.

Kord shook his head. "Nope. I don't play an instrument," he stated. A thought struck him, and he asked it. "Do you? Play an instrument, I mean?"

Mayvee shrugged. "Piano," she answered. "But only well enough to, like, accompany people singing Christmas carols at Christmas and stuff. Maybe the occasional soloist, if the piece isn't too hard."

"Wow!" Kord exclaimed. "Any other talents you'd like to share with me?"

Again Mayvee shrugged. "Not really," she said. She smiled, indicating something had come to mind.

"What?" Kord asked. "You thought of something else. What is it?"

"It's just something corny and stupid," she said, shaking her head in an effort to dismiss the thought.

"Tell me," Kord urged.

Mayvee rolled her eyes and blushed a bit. "Well, I'm a pretty fair yodeler."

Kord's eyes widened with astonishment. His handsome face lit up with an expression of admiration.

"Get out! Really?" he asked, chuckling.

"Yeah," Mayvee assured him.

"Let me hear it," Kord said.

Mayvee laughed, frowned, and said, "Here? In a diner?" She shook her head. "No way!"

"Well, at least tell me how you became a yodeler," Kord prodded. "I've never met a yodeler before."

Mayvee could see that he was truly interested. So shrugging once more, she began, "Well, the story of how I started yodeling is even dorkier than the fact that I *can* yodel."

"Yeah? So?" he said, nodding his head to encourage her to continue.

Exhaling a heavy sigh and wondering why she'd even mentioned her ability to yodel in the first place, Mayvee began, "I was eight years old when my aunt took me to see the *Sound of Music*...and that's when I was hooked."

"On yodeling?" Kord asked, his brows puckered quizzically.

Mayvee giggled. "Why am I not surprised that you don't get that? You're a boy, and typically boys aren't real big fans of movie musicals."

"Hey, I've seen it," Kord playfully defended himself, however. "I've had my share of being forced to watch certain movies with my mom and grandma, you know."

"Well, then do you remember the marionette scene in the movie?" she asked, baiting him.

"Yes, I do," he proudly said. "I saw the movie when I was about five, and the marionettes freaked me out so badly I had to sleep with my parents for two weeks."

Mayvee burst into laughter. She couldn't stop!

Kord frowned, feigning offence. "Hey! No laughing. Those things still creep me out."

"No, I know!" Mayvee agreed through her amusement. "I totally know what you mean! It's just…just so sad."

Kord's frowned reappeared. "It's sad…so you're laughing?" he teased.

Mayvee covered her mouth with one hand to try and stop her giggles.

"So…the goat puppet show in the *Sound of Music* started you yodeling, huh?" he asked.

Mayvee nodded. "Yeah. I started out just liking the song, but when I got to where I could really sing it well, including the yodeling, I totally loved the sensation in my throat when I yodeled. So I started yodeling other songs." She paused, "I mean, I'd never make it as Heidi in a Ricola commercial or anything. But I'm a fair yodeler, I guess…especially these days."

Kord was amazed. She yodeled? Just another unique and incredibly intriguing thing about the pretty Christmas tree decorator. And he couldn't wait to hear her do it.

"Now you," Mayvee said then.

"Me?" Kord asked, feigning ignorance.

"Yeah," she confirmed. "You don't play an instrument, and you don't yodel." She smiled at him, adding, "And believe it or not, I find that attractive for some reason."

I find you attractive, Kord thought to himself. "Whew! Thank goodness! I'd hate to think I'd lost my chances because I don't play the piccolo or yodel, you know?"

A twinkle of delight leapt into her eyes, and Kord was encouraged. It seemed she liked the idea of him wanting a chance with her.

"So? Other than being a phenomenal aquarium builder, setter-upper, and maintainer—not to mention a successful business owner—what do you like to do? You know, when you're stressed and stuff?"

"You mean, like, to chill myself out?" Kord asked, just for clarification.

"Yeah," Mayvee assured him.

She was momentarily distracted by his lips—the perfectly masculine shape of them, the two flawlessly symmetrical points at the top of his upper lip, the fullness, yet not too full shape, of his lower lip.

"Well, if you want to know the truth," Kord began as Mayvee watched his alluring lips move as he spoke, "I like to sort coins."

"You do?" she asked. "Like, you mean, look for wheat-back pennies or something?"

Kord shrugged. "Yeah, that too, I guess. I like to go to the bank and get rolls of pennies, dimes, nickels, quarters, even those new president dollars, and then mix them up in a big jar and sort them out into stacks by mint, year…like that. I do keep an eye open for wheat-backs, silver quarters, and dimes and coins minted before 1950 for some reason. It's just kind of brainless and helps me relax. You know?"

Mayvee smiled. "Well, how cute is that, Kord Derringer?" she exclaimed. "And it sounds very therapeutic."

"It is," he said, taking a drink from his glass. "So I sort coins. But if I'm really stressed and needing a break…" He paused, and Mayvee sensed he'd decided he didn't want to tell her what he'd started to.

"What?" she urged. "Come on! Tell me what else you do when you're too stressed for coin sorting to settle you down."

Mayvee was delighted when she noticed how Kord's cheeks pinked up a bit with a manly blush. "Go on. Spill the beans," she giggled.

He shrugged again and almost mumbled, "I'm a Lego geek."

Mayvee quietly squealed with delight, clapping her hands together as she laughed, "I love that! I totally love that!" She looked at him, wide-eyed with admiration and asked, "How big of a Lego geek are you?"

"Pretty big," he admitted, still blushing a bit. "Big enough that my house has a two-car garage, but one whole side is dedicated to my…my works of art."

"Really?" Mayvee asked, amazed.

Kord nodded. "Yep…really," he admitted.

Suddenly, Mayvee felt a bit like an underachiever. Apparently Kord owned his own home, and it was obvious he owned his own business. Mayvee wondered if he'd think she was a total loser when—once their dinner date was finished—she had to have him drop her off at her parents' home, instead of a place of her own.

She figured it would be better to let him know she was still on her parents' housing dime before he found out when he dropped her off. So she blurted, "Well, talents aside, I guess I'll be the first to lay the shortcomings card on the table and confess I still live with my parents. I mean, tuition is so expensive these days, and—"

"Why would you think that's a 'shortcomings' card, Mayvee?" Kord unexpectedly interrupted. "It's smart to live at home while you're in school, if you can. It helps you to avoid—"

"Student loan debt," Mayvee finished for him. She felt as if a burden of some weird kind of secret guilt had been lifted from her.

Kord shrugged. "I lived with my parents my whole four years of college," he explained. "And not only did I save on tuition, I saved enough to start my business and get into a house of my own." He grinned at her, his blue-green eyes smoldering with sudden allure. "You're gonna have to try a lot harder than that to find a shortcomings card to lay on my table of opinion of you."

Mayvee was the one blushing now, delighted by his understanding and implication that he approved of her.

"Still," he began then, "if we're going to lay out our shortcomings cards, right there next to our incredible talents of yodeling and Lego building..." he began.

Mayvee giggled, and he winked at her, sending goose bumps traveling over her arms and legs—awed that Kord could cover her in goose bumps with just a wink or a smile.

"Have you figured it out yet?" he asked.

"What? Figured what out?" Mayvee asked in return. "I thought we were sharing our shortcomings. What was I supposed to figure out?"

Kord smiled. "That I'm too lame to even have the guts to have just walked up to you and asked you out. No! I had to drive over to the tree lot and hire you to decorate a Christmas tree that I hadn't even purchased yet…just to get you to agree to have dinner with me."

Mayvee was blissful in the sudden joy of having what she thought was her imagination confirmed to be truth. She could hardly breathe! Kord really had purchased the ornaments and things *after* he'd hired her to decorate his store Christmas tree!

"I thought you were just really fastidious about taking care of your ornaments or something," Mayvee confessed. "But then I began to wonder—you know, when all the boxes of ornaments looked like they'd never been opened and the loose ones still had price tags on them."

"So now you know I'm a chicken…as well as an idiot," Kord told her. "I was afraid if I just flat out asked you to dinner, you woulda turned me down cold."

"Why?" Mayvee asked in a giggle. She shook her head. "I can't believe you did that. I can't believe you paid me to decorate a tree you didn't even need. I should totally give you your money back!"

"No," Kord said, reaching across the table and taking her hand. "The tree will be great for business, honestly. I'm just really happy that you didn't send me packing when I asked you to have dinner with me."

"Believe me, I would never send you packing," Mayvee said, starting to tremble as his thumb caressed the back of her hand.

"Does that mean you'll go out with me again?" Kord asked. "Like, maybe if you have some time off next week, you could help me pound out my Christmas shopping or something? We could have breakfast for supper again afterward, like at IHOP?"

"You're asking me out on a second date? Even though you now know that I'm a—well, I'll just say it—even though you know that I'm a yodeler?" she teased.

Kord laughed. "Especially now that I know you're a yodeler."

"Then, of course, I would love to pound out your shopping and eat breakfast for supper with you," Mayvee said—though she was half afraid she was dreaming.

"Great," Kord said. "Name the day, and I'll pick you up—whisk you away to a lavish world of mall crowds and IHOP syrup caddies."

Mayvee laughed and noticed that her hand was numb from the warmth and wonder of his touch.

♥

Kord smiled and exhaled a sigh. "Thanks for coming to dinner with me," he said, "and for decorating the Christmas tree in my storefront," he added with a wink.

Mayvee smiled, allowed a little giggle to escape her throat, and responded, "Well, thank *you* for taking me to dinner…and for *hiring* me to decorate the Christmas tree in your storefront."

As his beautiful blue-green eyes lingered on her for a long moment, a slight quiver of delight traveled through her body

Mistaking her quiver for a shiver against the cold, Kord politely said, "I should let you go inside so you can warm up. It is pretty cold out tonight."

"I suppose it is," Mayvee sighed with disappointment. She didn't want to leave him. She wanted to stand outside on the front porch all night long and talk with him—just be with him.

She thought back on her first high school prom— and how Jacob Webber had kept her out on the front porch for nearly an hour as he tried to get up the nerve to kiss her good night. Of course, Mayvee had *wanted* Jacob Webber to kiss her, so she hadn't minded too much. Sadly, when he finally *did* work up the nerve to kiss her, Mayvee was disappointed when not one spark of excitement accompanied his kiss. It was one reason she never went out with Jacob again—because she couldn't see the point of dating a boy who didn't give her a "zing" when he kissed her. Sure, Jacob was a nice enough boy—a friend—and she'd hoped his kiss would give her a zing—but it hadn't.

Still, one thing she did know—if Kord ever kissed her, the zings she'd feel! Just the way he looked at her, studied her, as they stood on her parents' front porch— just his gaze was sending little zings ricocheting through her mind and body. She couldn't imagine what would happen if he ever actually did kiss her.

Then, almost as if he'd been reading her thoughts, Kord asked, "Do you ever let boys kiss you good night on the first date, Mayvee?"

Mayvee gulped with astonishment—blushed crimson with hope. Was he serious? Was he asking because he wanted to kiss her good night? She felt like she had been tossed back in time into high school—like she was sixteen again and anticipating her first ever kiss.

She felt perspiration began to gather at her hairline, even for the chill in the frosty air.

"W-well, it would depend on who the boy was, I s-suppose," she stammered. Kord leaned toward her, and she was suddenly overheated.

Kord grinned just a little—a grin of mischief and near seduction of sorts. "Well, what about me? If I'm the boy who wants to kiss you good night? Would you let *me* kiss you good night?"

"Totally," she managed to breathe.

Mayvee's face was hot-to-uncomfortable with anticipation, excitement, hope, and a long-forgotten sort of schoolgirl bashfulness. She felt silly at being so completely giddy. It wasn't like she hadn't been kissed before. She'd had boyfriends in high school and since she'd been in college, but this was different. Kord brought forth feelings, emotion, and desires the like she'd never experienced before. And in that moment, there was nothing she'd ever wanted more in all her life than for Kord Derringer to kiss her good night.

He smiled and leaned even closer to her.

Mayvee was nervous. Kord could tell she was nervous by the fact that her cheeks were as red as Christmas apples. He wondered if his nerves were as obvious to her as hers were to him. He hoped not. He wanted her to think he was as smooth and cool as he was trying to appear—and as calm. After all, he was the aggressor in the situation. He was supposed to be confident—certain that she would like it if he kissed her—but he wasn't.

He wanted to put his hands at her waist and feel the softness of her sweater on his palms. He wanted to pull her body against his and really lay one on her. But he knew he had to play his cards carefully. If his kiss were too aggressive, she might think he was a pervert and bolt and run. If his kiss were too uncertain and timid—or quick and soft with no guts—she might think he was a weenie-boy and still bolt and run. It was a lot of pressure guys had to deal with, that first kiss needing to be perfect—at least to Kord's way of thinking.

But he really liked Mayvee Ashton—really, really, *really* liked her. So he decided to just go with his instincts, and his instincts told him to be careful but mildly aggressive as well. He'd know in a second or two whether he'd blown it. Her reaction would be either positive—and she'd allow him to linger in kissing her, and hopefully kiss him back—or she'd step back with disgust.

Kord knew there was nothing to do but to go for it—so he did.

Mayvee's entire body broke into wave after wave of goose bumps as one of Kord's hands settled at her waist, the other sliding to one side of her neck, his thumb resting on her cheek. In that next rapturous moment, he kissed her perfectly! His kiss wasn't at all tentative, but it wasn't too demanding either. It was firm and flawlessly applied with just the right amount of the parting of his lips—and the necessary, though unspoken, lingering that hinted to her that he wanted reciprocation.

And so Mayvee reciprocated, meeting his parted lips with the like parting of her own, pressing her mouth to his as confidently as her self-uncertainty would allow. For a brief instant, such a deluge of excitement and titillation flooded her body, met with the burst of stars and igniting colors in her mind, that she thought she might faint. She was so overwhelmed with the pleasure Kord's kiss rained over her that she was afraid she would pass out!

Fortunately, however, the odd sensation of vertigo subsided, and Mayvee found that somehow during her moments of blissful dizziness, Kord had pulled her against his body and into a powerful embrace. More startling than the realization that Kord was holding her as they continued to kiss was the fact that Mayvee's arms had somehow found their way around Kord's broad shoulders in their own embrace of him.

He was so warm, the feel of his whiskers against her skin around her mouth so invigorating and reassuring of the fact that he really did like her. Kord Derringer was muscular—far more muscular than Mayvee had previously surmised from just looking at him. She could feel that he was! His chest, arms, and shoulders were so solid and defined; it caused her already unequaled physical attraction to him to soar beyond the atmosphere.

Kord was still holding back. Mayvee sensed his restraint, even as she sensed her own, and it made her happy.

Even for the mutual and very powerful attraction sizzling between them, he didn't press the intensity of their kisses to a higher degree of exchange, and far too soon he ended the kiss they were sharing, smiling at her and mumbling, "I don't want you to have to slap me on our first date, you know?"

Mayvee giggled. "I don't want you to have to slap *me* on our first date either," she teased.

Kord smiled, obviously pleased with her response to his reason for ending their kissing. "I guess I'll say good night then…let you get inside and get to sleep. I'm sure you have a very busy day tomorrow."

Mayvee nodded. "I do. I work all day, and then I have two tree decorating appointments tomorrow evening," she confirmed. Her lips were still tingling with the lingering pleasure of his kiss.

"So you're off Thursday then?" he asked.

"Yeah," Mayvee sighed. For the first time in her whole life, she was a little resentful of the tree lot taking up so much of her time.

"So can I pick you up for some mall chaos Thursday morning?" he asked—staring at her mouth and making her wish he would kiss her again.

"You can pick me up any time you want," Mayvee said.

Kord chuckled. "I'll let that one slide by. How about nine a.m. then? So we can have a full day?"

"Nine a.m. on Thursday it is," Mayvee confirmed. She still couldn't believe she was actually standing on her front porch with the gorgeous Kord Derringer. She couldn't believe he'd asked her out again. And she really couldn't believe that her arms and legs still felt like jelly because of the lingering effects of his kiss.

"Well then, I better let you go, before I…I better let you go." He leaned down, placing a kiss to her forehead. "Good night, Mayvee."

"Good night," Mayvee breathed.

Kord turned and headed down the front walkway toward his truck. He started to whistle "White Christmas"—whistle just the way her grandpa used to do when he was still alive, just the way Bing Crosby had. It warmed her heart—caused even more feelings of approval, desire, and admiration toward Kord to well up inside her.

Kord got into his truck, started it, and waved to her, indicating she should enter the house. She waved at him and then turned, unlocked the door, and stepped in. Closing the door behind her, she peered out the small round window next to it, watching him drive away.

Closing her eyes and leaning back against the door for a moment, Mayvee breathed, "Merry Christmas to me!"

CHAPTER SIX

"New bras," Mayvee said, reaching into the bag of caramel corn as Kord offered it to her again.

"How can you tell?" Kord asked.

Mayvee shrugged. "Because she's coming out of Dillard's but she's not carrying one of those plastic garment bags they give you when you buy clothes, and she's not carrying one of those small bags from the makeup counters. And yet it's a smallish sort of bag. So it's obvious—new bras."

Kord chuckled. "Okay, I'll bite. But is she buying new bras for herself? Or are they a gift for someone, like her mom?"

He glanced to Mayvee—smiled with amusement as he watched her eyes narrow as she studied the tall, slender, very well put together woman that had just exited the mall entrance to Dillard's.

"They're for herself," Mayvee answered. "She wouldn't buy bras for her mom because she's an attorney and attorneys don't buy gifts for anybody but themselves." She shrugged, adding, "Or maybe occasionally for a client."

Kord nodded. "Okay. Wow, that's some insightful detective work."

Mayvee smiled at him and sighed. "It's a gift."

Kord laughed again, leaned back on the bench, and ate a handful of caramel corn. He'd never enjoyed a trip to the mall so much. Actually, he'd never enjoyed a trip to the mall—at least to shop. But with Mayvee, the mall was like some new and exciting, entirely undiscovered culture.

Kord picked Mayvee up early that morning, and they'd headed to the mall to do Kord's Christmas shopping. Much to his gladness, he'd soon discovered that Mayvee wasn't much into actually shopping, and she kind of looked at shopping the way he did—as a chore. However, he also soon discovered that she had ways of making the chore a bit more fun, and "people watching" was one of the ways she did it.

Furthermore, Mayvee didn't just people watch the way most mall bench-sitters did. She didn't sit and criticize or make fun of people. Instead, she expended her brainpower on guessing what shoppers had in their bags or pointing out the amusing antics of little kids. Mayvee seemed to derive a ton of entertainment by just sitting on a mall bench and watching the world go by— watching mall patrons and making elaborate guesses as to what they were purchasing.

It didn't take very long for Mayvee to draw Kord into enjoying her style of people watching. For one thing, it was very interesting, but mostly it was just incredible to be with her and to listen to her guesses.

"Okay," Mayvee said, "now you. You pick someone. Look! There's a guy coming out of that electronics store. What do you think he bought?"

Mayvee watched as Kord's eyes narrowed. She couldn't help but smile at him; he was so gorgeous after all! He was fun to be with too—really fun! He'd jumped right into her game of guessing what people had in their shopping bags. And he was good at it—cleverer than anyone she'd ever played it with before.

He munched on a few pieces of the caramel corn they'd purchased and then said, "A sound machine. You know, one of those little things you plug in and then it makes white noise or ocean sounds and stuff so you can sleep better."

Mayvee smiled with admiration. "Who is he buying it for? Himself?" she asked.

"Nope," Kord answered. He looked at her, winked, smiled, and said, "He's not an attorney, so he does buy gifts for people other than himself or his clients. He bought it as a gift for his wife because he snores a lot and it's been keeping her awake at night." He paused, arched his eyebrows in an expression of approval, and added, "In truth, it's a very thoughtful gift—the gift of a good night's sleep, you know?"

Mayvee giggled—delighted, amazed, and awash with admiration. "You are so good at this!" she complimented. "I've never had anyone play this with me that was so good at it…not even my brothers."

"Really?" Kord asked. "How about other guys…you know, like old boyfriends or just random dates?"

Mayvee exhaled a sigh, rolling her eyes as a memory of Nick Stevens popped into her mind. "Ugh…no! I tried to do this once with this guy I was dating, and ugh! He was so not into it and so not imaginative." Mayvee paused, reached for a handful of caramel corn, frowned, and added, "I should've know that day, that very day— and the fact that he was such a jerk about just people watching for fun—I should've known that relationship was doomed." She paused for a moment, nibbled on a caramel corn kernel, and added, "You know what? I *did* know that day that he was a jerk and I shouldn't be dating him."

Kord shrugged and asked, "Then why'd you keep dating him? I'm guessing you did after that."

Mayvee nodded, trying to beat off the self-loathing that was rising in her as she thought back on her time dating and working with Nick. "For stupid reasons. He had talked me into getting my real estate agent's license." She shook her head and sighed with sudden and very thorough disappointment in herself. "And I had put so much of my time and money into it that I felt I *had* to be a real estate agent, you know? And Nick was kind of mentoring me through the whole process, even though I hated it. But it was a job, and I'd expended a ton of resources on it, so I felt obligated, you know? And Nick was helpful…at work, anyway."

Kord grinned with obvious understanding. "I think we've all been there—had a job we knew we just couldn't tolerate or endure for one reason or the other." He paused and then asked, "So what was it you didn't like about the real estate business?"

"Everything!" Mayvee admitted. "But mostly all the BS—you know, the bologna. I sort of liked helping people find their homes, but I hated the selling part. And then when the Ghoul Disclosure thing popped up with this one family, I just couldn't do it anymore."

"Ghoul Disclosure?" Kord asked. "Sounds… ghoulish."

Mayvee smiled at him, thankful he'd lightened her mood again. "Yeah, some states have it and some states don't. This one does. And it basically means that sellers aren't required to disclose deaths that have happened in or on a property if the death was over three years before."

Kord frowned. "Even violent deaths? Like murder?"

"Exactly," Mayvee confirmed. "I was working with this seller, and during a home invasion six years prior, the father of a family living there had been murdered. The seller had known about the murder when he purchased the home shortly afterward, but it had been, like, five years since he'd purchased the home, and he didn't want to reveal the fact that a murder had occurred there. Legally, he didn't have to. But I felt it was unethical not to tell the little family that was considering purchasing the home that there had been a murder there. First of all, I just thought they should know. And second of all, if they bought the house and then tried to sell it later and it came out that it was a murder house, their value would probably plummet, you know?"

Kord nodded. "It sounds like the Ghoul Disclosure is in place to protect people who would let a little family move into a murder house without knowing."

Mayvee exclaimed, "That's how I felt!"

"So? What did you do?"

"I quit…and called the family looking at the house and told them where to find an article on the Internet about the house's history," Mayvee answered. She smiled. "They didn't buy it, and I was out of a job."

Kord smiled and moved his arm to rest on the back of the bench behind Mayvee's shoulders. "I like your integrity, Mayvee," he said. "I admire it. It makes you even more beautiful."

Mayvee blushed and playfully slapped him on one arm. "If you're just trying to make sure I let you have the rest of the caramel corn, I had already decided that you could."

"No, I mean it," Kord reassured her. "It takes a lot of courage to quit your job—any job—especially these days. And I like the fact you quit it for the reasons you did." He paused and then asked, "How did Nick take it?"

"Not well," she answered. "But I didn't care, because by then I'd already figured out I'd been dating him for the wrong reasons, so I…stopped."

Kord chuckled. "You mean you broke up with him? You cut him loose? You sent him packing?"

She laughed. "Yep! All of the above."

"Sweet deal for me, right?" he flirted. He took a strand of her long blonde hair between his fingers where they rested at her shoulder. It felt like silk—better than silk.

"Oh, you really want the rest of that caramel corn, don't you?" she teased.

"I was actually wondering why you weren't, like, a certified nurse assistant or something—something that would put you in the field of caring for the elderly," Kord offered. "I watched you with that old man at the tree lot the night we met, and then the way you were so good and patient with my grandparents. It kind of surprises me that you don't do something like that."

Mayvee's mouth dropped open in astonishment. She couldn't believe how perfectly he'd pegged her.

"Wow! Do you have ESP or something?" she asked.

Kord shrugged. "No. Why?"

"I actually was a CNA," she confessed. "I took my courses during my last two years of high school and started working in a nursing home right after I graduated."

"Really?" Kord asked. "But…you didn't stay with it? Why?"

Mayvee sighed as she thought of the lovely, sweet elderly people she'd worked with her first two years out of high school—thought of their funerals.

"I couldn't handle the loss," she admitted. "It nearly broke my heart every time one of our residents passed away. And then I lost all four of my grandparents during that time too, and I just couldn't do it anymore. I couldn't fall in love with people, just to lose them so quickly and so often, you know?"

Kord's beautiful blue-greens narrowed with understanding and sympathy. "I hadn't thought of that. That *would* be rough."

Mayvee shrugged. "Yeah. I just couldn't take the loss…and admittedly, just watching people suffer and slowly slip away wasn't something I found endurable either." She forced a smile and said, "So now I know two things I'm not cut out for—the medical field and real estate."

"Mayvee?" a familiar voice said from behind the bench.

"Oh no," Mayvee whispered.

"What? Are you doing your people watching thing again?" the same voice chuckled.

Mayvee was a little surprised when Kord stood up from his seat on the bench and turned to face Nick.

"Let me guess," Kord began. "Nick, right?"

Mayvee stood as well and turned around to see Nick standing there, all spiffed up in one of his expensive suits. Nick was tall, dark, and handsome as well—but not as tall or even nearly as handsome as Kord. Neither was his hair as dark. Looking from Kord to Nick and back, Mayvee wondered how she could've ever been any sort of attracted to Nick. Good-looking or not, he was a total putz!

Nick smiled and offered a hand to Kord. He looked to Mayvee and said, "I must have left a real impression, eh, Mayvee?"

"Yeah," Mayvee said as Kord rather unwillingly accepted Nick's handshake. "But not necessarily a good one."

Nick smiled and said, "Aw, be nice, Mayvs. You dumped me, remember?" He looked to Kord and asked, "Are you the newest victim of Mayvee's middle-class charm, man?"

"Actually, I'm hoping she'll be the victim of mine," Kord said, his voice low and somehow threatening. "Now, take off, man. And have a merry Christmas."

Nick's eyebrows arched in mild astonishment. "Whoa! Mayvs! I guess you're going in for the brooding, rugged type now, huh?"

In truth, Mayvee's heart was pounding so hard inside her chest, she thought it might rattle her brains! It wasn't because an old boyfriend had showed up but rather because the man she hoped would one day be her new boyfriend wasn't willing to take even the slightest bit of bull from the old one.

Forcing a smile at Nick, Mayvee said, "Yeah, I gave up jerks a while back. Merry Christmas, Nick."

She turned her back to him then—ignored him when he sarcastically mumbled, "Merry Christmas to you, Mayvee."

Kord didn't turn back around for several more moments, however. And when he did, his brow puckered as he said, "Now…what were we talking about before that ghoul showed up, hmmm?"

Smiling with pure pleasure and pride, Mayvee wrapped her arms around one of Kord's muscular ones and said, "We were talking about the plight of the elderly, and I was about to introduce you to my other favorite shopping mall game—the one I only play at this time of year…the one I save up all year to play."

"You save up to play?" Kord asked, smiling at her. "What? You're an arcade junkie or something?"

Mayvee giggled. "Nope. But I am a war veteran junkie, as well as a little-old-ladies-who-are-Christmas-shopping junkie!"

"And the explanation to that answer is…" Kord prodded, still confused.

"I have this big, old pickle jar at home," Mayvee began, "and every year I put all my change in it when I get home at night. Then I roll it, and…" She paused for a moment, remembering something Kord had told her earlier. "Wow! You would love my change jar!"

"I would," Kord confirmed. "So you roll all your change and…"

"And I get bills for it—fives, tens, and twenties—and then I come to the mall or go to the grocery store or something, and I give it to little old ladies that I see who are out Christmas shopping…most likely on a fixed budget. Or if I see a little old war veteran proudly wearing his veteran hat, I tell him, 'Thank you so much for your service, sir. Merry Christmas!' and I give him a bill."

"Wow!" Kord quietly exclaimed with obvious admiration. "That's pretty…that's incredible."

"Not really," Mayvee said. "I just remember once when I was a teenager, I saw this lady in Wal-Mart—an elderly lady—and she was in the jewelry section, and she was digging through her little coin purse to see if she had enough money to purchase a pair of cheap earrings. My mother accidently bumped into her and apologized. The lady looked at me and said, 'You look to be about the same age as my granddaughter. Do you think she would like these earrings?' I looked at the earrings, and they were pretty…and only cost four dollars. I told her they were really lovely and that I was sure her granddaughter would love them. She thanked me and told us that she hoped she had enough change to purchase them. I felt sick to my stomach with feeling so bad for her. I wanted so badly for her to get the little earrings for her granddaughter…but I didn't have any money." She paused, feeling the large lump of anxiety rise to her throat—the lump that had risen in her throat every time she thought of that old lady since the day it happened.

"Well?" Kord urged. "Did she have enough change for them?"

"No," Mayvee said. "And I was heartbroken. Until I saw my mother do something that is so, so, so, so my mother…and so kind. As the look of disappointment— of crushing disappointment—took over the old woman's face and as she started to put the earrings back, my mom exclaimed, 'Oh wait! It looks like you dropped something, ma'am.' I saw her pull some change and a folded five-dollar bill out of her coat pocket and drop it at the lady's feet. The little old lady was so excited! Her face lit up as bright as the Christmas star as she saw the money at her feet. I don't even think she suspected my mom at all and just picked up the money, thanked my mom for having such sharp eyes, and headed to the register to buy the little pair of earrings for her granddaughter."

Mayvee paused, trying to sniffle back the tears in her eyes and the emotions in her throat. Then she continued, "I've never forgotten that moment—not the little old lady's kind, loving heart and desire to do something for her granddaughter, and not my mom's incredible insight and giving spirit." She shrugged. "It may sound ridiculous, but I think that moment helped shape me, you know? It was just a moment—just one little thing out of a million that happens—but it changed me."

Kord swallowed the lump of emotion that had risen to his throat as he'd listened to Mayvee tell her story. It was a deeply good character that could be so influenced by such a fleeting, albeit profound moment in life.

"So now you hunt for little old ladies and gentlemen to give to, huh?" Kord almost mumbled. He looked at Mayvee, hoping she could see the sincere admiration in his eyes. "That's about the most awesome thing I've ever heard. It's like those videos people post of themselves paying for people's groceries and stuff." He paused as his admiration for Mayvee continued to grow. "Only you don't film, do you?"

Mayvee laughed. "Heck no! If you do something kind for someone and then film it yourself to blast it out to the world…" She shrugged. "I don't know. To me that seems like you're just looking for compliments and glory, you know? I mean, what about the person you're doing it for? Maybe it's embarrassing for them, you know?" Again she shrugged. "I just think…well, if you're really doing something to help someone or to make them feel loved and appreciated, it should be done with as little attention from others as possible. I mean, my mom could've just offered to give the lady the extra money, but how more wonderful was it for the little lady to just think she really had had enough money all along? Giving her the money might have taken away some of her joy in buying the earrings herself for her granddaughter, you know?"

Kord shook his head, awed by Mayvee's selfless way of thinking. "You're incredible," he said.

"No, no, no," Mayvee kindly argued, however. "I'm not incredible. I just think it's something we all should do, you know? We should do it all year long, but I choose to do it now, because I know elderly people have giving hearts and are on fixed incomes. I just want them to have enough in their coin purse to buy a little inexpensive pair of earrings for their granddaughters, you know?"

The force of emotions broiling inside Kord's chest were something he'd never experienced before—admiration, astonishment, marvel, awe! "Wow," he breathed. "I mean, I buy a fast food meal here and there for a homeless person, and I admit to being more conscious of doing that this time of year…but wow!" He gazed at her for a long moment. "This is in your soul, isn't it?"

Mayvee shrugged, hugged his arm more tightly, and said, "Yeah, I guess so. I always just wish I had more change saved up, you know?"

"Well, how much do you have…if you don't mind my asking?" Kord inquired.

"Two hundred and seventy dollars, in various denominations of paper bills," she proudly announced.

Mayvee smiled with curiosity as Kord reached around to his back pocket and withdrew his wallet. Unfolding it and looking in the cash section, he silently counted the bills inside.

"I've got two hundred and forty-seven on me," he said, flashing his dazzling smile down at her. "Let me contribute to the fun, okay?"

"Oh, you don't have to do that!" Mayvee exclaimed, suddenly afraid he thought she was bragging or hinting for more money for her cause. "I-I just wanted to share the fun with you. I didn't mean to make you feel like you had to—"

"But I want to!" Kord exclaimed. "As long as you don't feel like I'm stepping on your toes or something. This way we can have twice as much fun for twice as long, you know?"

"Well…if you really want to," Mayvee said. Thinking of the load of gifts they had put in Kord's truck not long before, she added, "But you already spent so much doing your Christmas shopping and stuff. I don't want you to feel like…"

But Kord shook his head. "Oh, that's a completely different thing," he said. "This sounds like so much more fun…satisfying too, you know?"

"Yeah, I do," she admitted.

Shoving his wallet back into his pocket, Kord said, "Okay, then. Let's get started. But first…"

Mayvee gasped when, right there in the middle of the mall, Kord took her face between his hands, pressing his mouth to hers in a very unyielding, concentrated, toe-tingling, zinging kiss! He kissed her this way several times in succession, turning her knees to jelly.

Still holding her face in his hands, he looked at her—his blue-green eyes sparkling with admiration—saying, "You're amazing, Mayvee. I've never known anyone like you."

Mayvee smiled, feeling rather delirious and dizzy. "Thanks…I guess."

Kord nodded, took hold of her hand with one of his, and said, "Let's get to it, shall we? Let's spread some of that unique Christmas cheer that only you can spread."

"That only *we* can spread," Mayvee playfully corrected.

Her hand was so warm where it was clasped in his strong, callused one, and Mayvee rather enjoyed the jealous glances she received from some other young women as she and Kord walked through the mall looking for possible candidates to wish a merry Christmas to.

She was amazed at how readily he'd jumped into her game of seeking out the elderly and trying to cheer them a bit, how eager he was to match her own funds with his so that they could do more and for longer. Furthermore, Mayvee's feet felt as if she were walking on air—a physical sensation left as a blissful consequence of his having kissed her. He'd kissed her—again! She could hardly believe it.

Yet as Kord nodded toward a nearby elderly gentleman, walking with a cane and wearing a WWII ball cap, Mayvee was so very glad she'd chosen to take the risk of letting Kord in on her secret Christmas tradition. She could tell he was just as excited at the prospect of making someone smile and feel noticed as she was.

"Let's stalk him a bit first," Mayvee whispered. "You know, see if he goes anywhere to purchase anything or maybe even to the food court for a snack. Then when the moment is right, we'll strike!"

Mayvee was rendered breathless for a moment when Kord reached out, cradled her chin in his free hand, and kissed her once more. "You're so awesome!" he told her.

CHAPTER SEVEN

As they drove home from the mall, Mayvee just couldn't keep from staring at Kord. After all, she had an awesome view from her place in the passenger's seat of his truck. She couldn't keep from thinking about the fact that Kord had so thoroughly enjoyed giving to people that night—and not just to the elderly men and women they had sought out and given small gifts of cash to. After they'd rather quickly blown through their combined cash, Kord hadn't been satisfied. And so they'd gone to the food court in the mall, where he'd purchased ten meals from the sandwich shop. Then they'd hopped in his truck and headed to nearby downtown to distribute the meals to the first ten homeless people they'd happened upon. Of course, Kord had made certain they only ventured into well-lit areas, and only after he'd spoken to a parked police officer to inquire as to who might most be in need and where they would be. It had been a profound experience for Mayvee—something beyond even her own Christmas fun of giving to the elderly. She found that giving food to those in such dire straits and in such great need came with an entirely different sort of humbling—and she was grateful for it.

Mayvee had never met a man like Kord Derringer. His desire to give and make others happy was sincere— entirely genuine. Oh, she knew many men and women who were caring, giving, sympathetic, and empathetic of others—especially those in need. Yet Mayvee found that Kord was truly in like thinking with her. As she noticed the plight of the elderly and suffered for them, so he was sensitive to the homeless and their hunger and misery.

Therefore, Mayvee found it difficult not to simply stare at Kord in admiring awe of not only his gorgeous face and physique but also his depth of spirit and compassion. Mayvee couldn't think of another man she'd ever known who was as rugged and manly as Kord, yet with a heart of gold beating inside his broad, muscular chest. He was incredible, and she kept wondering what in the world she had done to capture his attention.

"I know it's getting late, and you're probably completely worn out and sick of me," Kord began, rattling Mayvee from her thoughts of admiration of him. "But would you mind if we stopped by my grandparents' house on the way to yours? I had promised I'd swing by tonight at some point, and I know they'd love to see you again. Would you mind?"

Kord glanced over at her, smiling, and Mayvee knew she would never be able to refuse him anything!

Especially if he flashed that dazzling smile at her every time he asked.

"I don't mind at all," she assured him. After all, she'd gladly jump at any excuse to linger in his company for a while longer.

"Thanks," Kord said. "I think they get extra lonesome this time of year—you know, with all their kids grown up and even most of their grandkids. You know?"

"I do know," Mayvee said. She sighed with missing her own grandparents. "I wish I could have spent more time with my grandparents…all of them. I miss them every day, but it's worse at Christmastime, for some reason."

"I can imagine that it is," Kord said.

He turned the truck down a familiar street, and Mayvee felt her heart lighten again when she saw the beautiful Christmas tree gleaming in the familiar bay window.

"Well, I guess they liked it enough to leave it up, huh?" she thought out loud.

"What, the tree?" Kord asked. He chuckled. "Believe me, they love it! Grandma tells me how beautiful it is every time I talk to her. I really made some brownie points by getting you to do their tree this year."

"It's the lights you put on the tree and the ornaments your grandma collected over the years that make it so beautiful," Mayvee reminded him. "I just slapped them on there, that's all."

Kord looked at her and winked. "Hey, take credit where credit is due, Mayvee. You did a beautiful job!

And besides, Grandma says the ornament spinners you added are her favorite thing about the tree this year."

"Well, I'm glad she's pleased," Mayvee said. "I just love Christmas trees! If I'm ever incredibly wealthy, I'm going to have a guestroom in my house that has a rustic, cabin-type feel…complete with a Christmas tree in one corner that I can enjoy all year long."

Kord couldn't keep from smiling as he glanced at Mayvee. She was so kind, so cute, so adorable—so pretty in her fuzzy red sweater. The truth was, Kord had never enjoyed a Christmas season as an adult the way he'd been enjoying this one. But with Mayvee— well, she made everything about Christmas seem more wonderful, more heartfelt, more what it should be about in the first place.

He knew he would never forget the expressions on the faces of the people to whom they'd given their small gifts of "mad money" (as Mayvee called it). Tired, foggy eyes suddenly lit up with a new sparkle—a recognition that someone, strangers, cared. The fact of the matter was that Kord had felt moisture rise in his eyes on several occasions when he and Mayvee had given away their meager but loving offerings. Elderly people still had class, appreciation, and manners. They'd lived through hard times—the Great Depression, wars, food rationing—therefore they truly valued a kind thought more than money.

Furthermore, watching Mayvee's joy at helping people had been an incredible experience in itself. And Kord had also been glad that he'd been able to show her the plight of the homeless a little more closely and how one simple meal could make a person feel important as well.

All in all, it had been one of the most dramatic, life-changing, and wonderful nights of Kord's entire life—and he had the beautiful Christmas tree lot girl to thank for it. She was settling herself into his heart and his soul; he could feel it. A hope in life—and excitement in the adventures in living that it would bring—had begun to expand inside him, all because of Mayvee.

Kord pulled into his grandparents' driveway. There was another car in the driveway—a black SUV.

"Is someone else here?" Mayvee asked as her nerves began to rattle a little.

"Oh, that's just my dad's car," Kord said, as if it were the most casual thing in the world.

"Your dad's car?" Mayvee squeaked. "Um…I don't want to impose on a family thing," she stammered.

"It's just my mom and dad, Mayvee," Kord explained, as if there were nothing at all unusual about bringing Mayvee into a family gathering at his grandparents' home. "I guess they'll get to meet you tonight."

Mayvee gulped. "But…but are you sure we should…that I should be here? I mean…"

Kord turned off the truck's engine, reaching over to cup her chin in one hand. "Hey, didn't I already meet your mom? And your brothers? It's only fair that you meet my parents, right?"

"That's different, and you know it," Mayvee playfully argued.

But when Kord leaned over, kissing her quickly, once again Mayvee's knees liquefied.

"Not much," he said, winking at her. "Hold on, and I'll get your door."

Kord was out of the truck then and walking to her side of it.

"His parents?" Mayvee whispered to herself. "Tonight?" she breathed, knowing that, after an entire day at the mall shopping, she probably looked like something the cat dragged in!

All too quickly for her nerves, Kord opened the passenger's side door. "Come on. Let's go in. I want to show you off to my mom and dad."

"I'm not much to show off...especially right now," Mayvee said, taking his hand as he helped her step down out of the truck.

"You're the most beautiful woman I've ever known, Mayvee," Kord said. His voice was low and sincere, his blue-green eyes narrowed and smoldering with emotion.

Mayvee's heart began to pound inside her chest. Kord was magnificent! He was everything she'd ever dreamt of finding in a man. Kord Derringer was her Mr. Right!

As Kord leaned down, intending to kiss her again, Mayvee held her breath—stiffened her knees so that when they turned to jelly (and she knew they would), she wouldn't lose her balance.

But the sound of the front door to his grandparents' home opening interrupted Kord's intentions to kiss her.

"Hey there, kids! We saw you drive up," his grandpa chuckled as he came down the front porch steps toward them.

"Hi, Grandpa," Kord greeted.

He hugged his grandpa, and Mayvee hugged him too.

"It's so good to see you again, Mayvee," George greeted.

"You too, Mr. Derringer," Mayvee returned.

George put an arm around her shoulders, chuckled, and said, "It's George, remember? Or why not just Grandpa? That'll make it even easier. Come on in! We're firing up the griddle for some French toast if you kids are hungry."

"They're always eating breakfast over here," Kord said, taking Mayvee's hand.

"Well, you know what your Grandma always says. Pancakes and bacon: because life is just too short to eat bran flakes for breakfast!"

Mayvee laughed as Kord pointed out, "But it's suppertime, Grandpa."

George tossed a dismissing wave in the air. "Breakfast, lunch, supper—all meals are better with pancakes or French toast on the menu."

Gulping the huge lump of anxiety that had risen in her throat, Mayvee stepped into the Derringers' home. George and Kord followed her inside, closing the door behind them. She was trapped! There was no escaping meeting Kord's parents now—no matter what she looked like.

"Martha!" George called. "Kord and his girlfriend are here!"

"Girlfriend?" Mayvee heard a feminine voice exclaim from the other room. "What girlfriend?"

In the very next instant, a beautiful middle-aged woman and a very handsome, Kord-looking middle-aged man appeared from the other room. Kord's parents were staring at Mayvee like she had Queen Victoria's crown sitting on top of her head.

"Kord Derringer!" the woman exclaimed. "Why haven't we met this pretty angel?" Hurrying toward Mayvee, Kord's mother smiled as she said, "Kord, introduce us to your girl here, please."

"Mom, this is Mayvee Ashton," Kord said without pause. "Dad, this is Mayvee. Mayvee, this is my mom and dad, Elly and Michael Derringer."

"We're so pleased to meet you, Mayvee," Mrs. Derringer nearly squealed as she clasped Mayvee's hand in a warm greeting.

"We certainly are," Mr. Derringer said with an understanding wink.

"Mayvee here is the little fairy that did up your mother's tree so nicely, Mike," George said to Kord's father.

"Oh! And it is beautiful, Mayvee," Elly exclaimed— and sincerely. "When I saw Martha's tree, I was overwhelmed. It's just beautiful!"

"Have you kids been out today?" Mike asked his son.

Mayvee smiled, noting that Kord's father owned the same mischievous grin Kord did.

"Yep," Kord answered. He put an arm around Mayvee's shoulders as a show of support and protection—and she loved it! "Mayvee helped me bang out my Christmas shopping today."

"Oh, shopping with Kord," Elly began. "You're a brave girl. And I guess you've figured out that Kord does *not* like to shop."

"Yeah," Mayvee admitted. "And it worked out really well, because I'm not a fan of shopping either."

"This one's a keeper, Kord," Mike said. "A woman who doesn't like to shop? I didn't know there was such a thing." He kissed his wife as she playfully slapped him on the chest.

"Well, come on in, kids," George urged. "Your grandma is in the kitchen." Kord's grandpa winked at Mayvee, licked his lips, and said, "I love French toast for supper."

Everyone turned back toward the kitchen, and Mayvee was glad Kord kept his arm around her shoulder.

"They think I'm your girlfriend," Mayvee whispered, blushing.

But Kord simply shrugged. "So? Is there a problem with that?"

Mayvee looked up at him—saw the admiration and pleasure in his countenance.

"W-well…not if you don't think there is," she stammered.

Kord smiled, said, "I definitely don't," and began pulling her toward the kitchen with him.

Mayvee couldn't feel her feet moving—even though she was moving toward the kitchen. Was he kidding? Could it really be possible that Kord didn't care if his parents mistook her for his girlfriend? Or even more inconceivable, was his implication that of her seriously having a chance of one day being his girlfriend?

"Kord, you've brought Mayvee!" Martha exclaimed as Kord and Mayvee stepped into the kitchen. "How fabulous! How many pieces of French toast will you eat, Mayvee honey?"

♥

"You poor little thing," Kord laughed as he pulled up in front of Mayvee's parents' home three hours later. "You totally looked like you'd been ambushed. I'm so sorry. I really didn't think they'd make such a big deal."

"It's all right," Mayvee said. "It was really fun, and your parents are so awesome! Plus, I think your grandma really does like the decorating job I did on her tree, and that makes me happy."

"Of course she likes it," Kord affirmed, putting the truck in park. He did, however, turn the engine off, and Mayvee was glad—because she figured it meant he wasn't in a big hurry to leave yet.

"You did a perfect job," Kord assured her. "I mean, my mom even asked you if she could hire you to do hers next year. And believe me, *that's* a compliment." He smiled at her. "You're something extra special…you know that, right?"

Mayvee blushed, even though she was thoroughly delighted by the compliment. "Aw, anybody can throw ornaments up onto a Christmas tree."

"That's not what I mean," Kord said. His smile faded a little as his eyes narrowed. He was very serious as he said, "I have never had a day like today, Mayvee…never. You really do know what the Christmas spirit is all about."

"So do you," Mayvee reminded him. "Don't try to play all dumb, like giving meals to the homeless isn't an incredibly compassionate thing to do."

But Kord shook his head. "Yeah, but today…the whole day was incredible," he said. "I even enjoyed the shopping part, and believe me, that's a miracle in itself." He reached out, taking her hand and pulling it to his lips. "It was because of the company I was in…the reason I enjoyed the shopping, you know."

Hot, wonderful goose bumps began at the tips of Mayvee's fingers of the hand Kord was holding, traveling up her hand, over her arm to her neck, and all the way to her head. Even her hair follicles were tingling from his touch!

"Well, I'm glad you enjoyed it, because I had the most wonderful time of my life…and I'm not kidding," she confessed, her blush deepening with her own brazenness.

"Can I take you to dinner tomorrow night when I get off from work?" Kord asked. "Or do you not take a dinner break this time of year?"

Mayvee's heart nearly melted with joy. "You mean, being with me all day and most of the night tonight didn't burn you out on my company?"

Kord shook his head. "Nope. Not at all."

Mayvee sighed with blended happiness and disappointment. "I would love to go to dinner with you, but unless you want to brown bag it at the tree lot with me, I can't. I'm on the night shift tomorrow—the all-night night shift—as in all night and overnight night shift."

"The overnight night shift?" Kord asked, wrinkling his handsome brows.

"Yeah. With Dad away, the rest of us have to take turns staying at the lot overnight—you know, for security and stuff," Mayvee explained. "Dad used to do it, but now, we all have to step up, you know?"

Kord's curious expression turned into that of concern. "You stay there all night…alone?"

Mayvee shrugged. "I'll probably get Josh to stay with me or a friend or something," she explained. "So I won't be *all* alone." She bit her lip with trepidation, wondering if she should even mention the thought that had just popped into her mind. "You…you wouldn't like to come by and have something to eat with me at the tree lot after it closes, would you?" she decided to venture. "I mean, it wouldn't be fancy—probably something microwavable—but we could watch a movie or something…or just have popcorn if you don't want to eat that late or—"

"I'll be there," Kord interrupted. "Just tell me what time."

"Really?" Mayvee asked. She was kind of stunned that he'd accepted her invitation so immediately. "I mean, you don't think I'm too forward for asking *you* to dinner instead of waiting until you maybe might ask me again…"

Mayvee gasped with instant euphoria as Kord leaned over the truck's center console, pressing a very firm, very warm kiss to her mouth.

"On the contrary," he answered. "I'm glad you did. It gives me hope that maybe you like me as much as I like you."

Mayvee sighed with further elation. "Okay. Wanna come by about midnight, just before I close the lot then?"

"You bet," Kord said, kissing her again.

It was warm inside the cab of the truck—warm because Kord had kissed Mayvee twice and was looking at her like he wanted to kiss her again.

"This was the one of the best days of my life, you know," she confessed to him. "I've never had a day like this before, a day I just don't want to end…ever."

Kord glanced at his watch. He looked back to Mayvee and said, "Well, it's eleven forty-five…so we've got fifteen minutes before this day is officially over. Wanna wait out that last fifteen minutes of today with me?"

"I'd love to," Mayvee agreed.

She smiled, her hair follicles starting to tingle again at the very first touch of his lips to hers. Kord slid his hands under her hair at the back of her neck as he began to deepen the intensity of their kiss. This kiss was different even from the fantasy-like kiss they'd shared the first time on the front stoop of Mayvee's house. It was different than the firm, determined, yet fairly quick kisses he'd given her several times that day. This kiss was more comfortable—more intimate—more hair-follicle-tingling, more zing-zing-zinging than any kiss Mayvee had ever experienced before—even from Kord!

Kord hands were large, strong, with callused palms from hard work, yet soft enough to feel good on her tender skin, and Mayvee relished his touch as his hands lingered at her neck as they kissed. His mouth was warm and moist, and the way he kissed her—like she was some decadent dessert he could never get his fill of—made Mayvee's heart beat so fast and furious, the sound echoed in her ears.

Mayvee reached up, pressing her hand against Kord's rugged, square, whiskery jaw. The feel of his jaw working as he kissed her—the realization that the most exquisitely attractive man she'd ever seen liked her and found her interesting—was kissing her—overwhelmed her to trembling with emotion.

Kord must've mistaken Mayvee's sudden trembling for a chill—for in the next moment he had wrapped her in the strength of his arms, against him, even for the fact that the center console should've made their embrace awkward. But it didn't, and Mayvee melted against him, relishing the fiery passion that was barely bridled by them both.

♥

Mayvee was somewhat disappointed to see Craig and Josh sitting on the couch watching some late night sit-com reruns when she walked through the front door. She'd wanted to be alone—to wander around the house, basking in the lingering bliss of her day with Kord—especially the last fifteen minutes of said day.

"Did you and Dagwood have yourselves a good time tonight?" Craig teased.

"Yes, we did," Mayvee answered. She studied her brothers a moment—both of whom looked like they'd had a very long, very hard day. Her heart softened toward them, for she knew how long and hard a busy day at the lot could be.

"Thanks for covering for me today, guys," she said. "It meant a lot, and I did have a great day…and night."

Josh smiled. "Yeah, we can tell by the whisker burn around your mouth."

"Yep. Looks like you and Dagwood had a good time decorating trees together, huh?" Craig teased.

Craig and Josh high-fived, chuckling, amused at their own wit.

Mayvee, however, rolled her eyes and said, "And here I was feeling sorry for you guys for having to run the lot all by yourselves today."

"Sorry, Mayvee," Josh said. "I really am glad you had fun…really."

"Me too, Blondie," Craig said. His expression was that of sincerity for once. "And I like this Kord guy, Mayvs. He seems, you know, like an upfront kind of guy. Manly too."

"He is," Mayvee agreed. "And I'm off to bed…to dream about him some more."

Craig and Josh both groaned and playfully rolled their eyes.

"Chicks, man," Craig said.

"I hear you, dude," Josh agreed.

"Good night, boys," Mayvee said.

Once inside her room, Mayvee turned on the lights of her personal Christmas tree. Ever since she was a little girl, Mayvee had had her own Christmas tree in her bedroom. It hadn't been at all hard to talk her parents into it. After all, Mayvee had begun wrapping rocks as Christmas gifts for people when she was only four years old—and in July. Even before the tree lot had become such an Ashton family institution, Mayvee had been in love with Christmas trees, Christmas, and gift-giving. She smiled as she studied her Christmas tree as she readied for bed. Then, stretching out on her bed to wind down, she gazed upon the glimmering tree—awed by the fact that Christmas trees held such magic and beauty.

In all her life, Mayvee had felt that a Christmas tree all lit up with lights and shiny ornaments was one of the most beautiful things in all the world. It was a sight that soothed her and brought her peace—lightened her heart when it was heavy, inspired hope in her when things seemed bleak. But now—now as she studied the lovely tree in her room, she realized that there were other things of such brilliant beauty as well, just a different sort of beauty—the brilliant light that leapt to an old lady's cloudy, cataract-afflicted eyes when someone reminded her that she was not forgotten and of immeasurable worth—the toothless smile of a homeless man when a warm meal was gifted him in kindness— and the incomparability and power of sudden, nearly instant, unexpected, and thoroughgoing love the like that Kord Derringer had sparked inside her.

She loved Kord; she was in love with him. After only a handful of hours with him, Mayvee knew she was already in love with Kord—that he was her proverbial Mr. Right. Was she crazy to think that she could already know for certain that he was the man she wanted to spend her life with—have children with? Probably—but she didn't care. Almost overnight, something had changed in her. In a matter of days, Mayvee had gone from having no direction regarding a permanent job and a vagueness of what she truly wanted in life to a certainty—a certainty that she wanted Kord Derringer for her own, forever, and that everything else in life, come what may, would be based on, and effloresce from, her love for him.

CHAPTER EIGHT

"Give me about an hour, Mayvs," Josh began. "I just need to scrub off some of this tree sap, e-mail my English Lit paper to my teacher, and I'll be back to stay with you tonight."

"Are you sure, Josh?" Mayvee asked her younger brother. "You have school tomorrow, and Mom won't want you too worn out."

But Josh smiled, placing a reassuring hand on Mayvee's shoulder. "I'm not going to let you stay here all night by yourself, Mayvee," he assured her. "And besides, I have late arrival tomorrow, so I don't have to be up at the crack of dawn or anything." Josh's smile broadened with understanding. "And don't worry. I'll come in through the back gate and sleep on the cot in the storage room so I don't interrupt your hot midnight date with Mr. Fish Tank, okay?"

Mayvee blushed. "I wasn't worried about that," she fibbed.

But Josh laughed. "Of course you were, you dork! You won't be able to get up your nerve to make out with him if your little brother is loitering around the whole time."

"I am not planning to make out with him," Mayvee giggled guiltily.

"Yeah, right, whatever," Josh teased. "Well, let's just say that I don't want to interrupt your deep, serious political conversations then. I'll be beat by the time I get back, so I'll just turn on the space heater and conk out. No spying on you and your Greek god, okay? I promise."

"Okay, thanks," Mayvee said, hugging her brother.

Josh hurried off toward the back entrance to the lot. The Ashtons always parked their cars in the small graveled area just outside the back entrance. As Mayvee watched her brother go, she admitted to herself that she hoped Kord arrived soon—not only because she wanted to be with him but also because it unsettled her to be all by herself at the lot.

Mere moments later, however, Mayvee saw Kord pull up in his truck. At once she was reassured about her own safety—*and* thrilled to the very tips of her toes at the prospect of spending time with him.

Kord's smile broadened as he walked toward Mayvee. She was wearing her worn jeans, little work boots, a baggy men's red flannel shirt over a black turtleneck T-shirt, and her long stocking cap over braided hair. She looked so much like she did the first time he'd met her—pretty, alluring, and absolutely adorable!

"Hi there," he said as Mayvee walked toward him, meeting him just inside the fence that surrounded the tree lot.

"Hi there, yourself," she greeted. She smiled and blushed a little, and Kord could not contain himself.

Reaching out to take her face between his hands, he kissed her, chuckling when a bit of tree sap on her lower lip caused her lip to stick to his for an instant when he pulled away. "Got a little tree sap on you today, I see," he said.

"Oh, I know," Mayvee groaned as she pressed the spot on her lower lip, grimacing as it stuck to her finger. She bit at the spot a little with her top teeth but then shrugged. "It's murder to get sap off, you know, especially when you get it on your face."

"I can imagine," Kord agreed. He thought of the movie *Christmas Vacation*—of Chevy Chase trying to flip through a magazine with tree-sapped hands—and he chuckled again.

"It's not funny," Mayvee giggled. "It'll take forever to wear off." He turned and watched as she closed the chain link fence gates behind him and used a chain and padlock to secure them together.

"So how was your day?" she asked as she walked back to him, linking her arm through his. Kord liked that she felt comfortable enough to link arms with him—although he *had* seen her do the same thing to an elderly man the first night he met her. Still, it felt wonderful to have her touch him—and for her to take the initiative again.

119

"Pretty busy, actually," he answered. "Everybody always waits until the last minute and then wants what they want in time for Christmas."

"So this is last minute for you already?" Mayvee asked.

"Yeah," Kord confirmed. "It takes time to do custom aquarium jobs…even to get specialty fish and plants in for regular aquariums, you know?"

"I do now," she said. "I guess I never thought about getting live fish for Christmas before."

"And how was business at the good old Christmas tree lot today?" Kord asked. Mayvee had led him to the fire pit, where a fire still burned low, but warm and soothing. She seemed to study the smoldering embers on the outer edge of the fire's center.

"Busy…thank goodness!" she responded. She looked up to him and smiled, adding, "Though the tree pooper pooped out for about an hour before Craig managed to get it working again, so we had to tie trees to the tops of cars the old-fashioned way." She reached up, touching her lower lip with one finger again. "I think that's when the sap got me."

Kord smiled at Mayvee, bent down, and kissed her again. He laughed when her lower lip did indeed stick to his a little again as he pulled away.

"Well, I kind of like your sappy lip," he told her. "It makes the kiss last longer, right?"

Mayvee blushed. "Right," she agreed. She nodded toward two of the old wooden lawn chairs sitting near the fire. "Wanna sit down for a while and watch the fire die out?" she asked.

"Yeah," Kord agreed. "I can't remember the last time I got to just sit around a fire and relax."

"I know," Mayvee said as she took a seat in one of the chairs. Kord sat down in the chair next to her, and she studied him a moment. He looked uber-cool in his caramel-colored barn coat, Levi's, and work boots. His cheeks and nose were a little red from the cold, and she noted how much the fact emphasized the light blue-green of his eyes.

"Ahhh," he sighed. "Now this is living."

Mayvee nodded in agreement. "I love this part of working at the tree lot—the smell of the wood burning, the crackle, and just getting to sit here after everyone's gone and unwind. It makes working the latest shift worth it."

She looked from the glowing fire to Kord. He was smiling at her and seemed to be studying her from head to toe.

"What?" she giggled self-consciously.

"Your hat," he said. "I'm assuming you know it looks just like the one—"

"That Randy wears in *A Christmas Story*?" she finished with another giggle. "That's because my grandma made it for me a few years ago—the year she passed away actually. It's my own little replica of Randy's stocking cap."

"Well, it looks great on you," Kord said. "Especially with your little braids hanging out from under it on each side."

Mayvee shook her head. "Yeah, after I asked you to meet me for dinner tonight, I didn't think of the fact that I'd look like a dirty old teamster by the time you got here."

"I like this look on you," he said, however. "Honestly, you're too adorable for words in your tree lot girl outfit." Kord reached over, taking hold of the yarn pom-pom on the end of her stocking cap and brushing it across her nose. "And the Randy stocking cap—it's like the crowning accessory, you know?"

"Oh, I'm sure it is," Mayvee said. But as she looked at him—bathed in the mesmerizing blue-green of his eyes—she could see that he was sincere.

"And speaking of Randy's stocking cap," Kord began, "I'm pretty good at movie trivia…especially *A Christmas Story* movie trivia."

"You are?" Mayvee asked, delighted.

"Yep," Kord assured her. "Ask me anything about it. You'll see."

"Okay," Mayvee said, taking the bait. "There is always something I've wondered. You know in the kitchen at breakfast in that one scene?"

"Yeah?" Kord prodded.

"And the Old Man is doing his crossword and asks about the Lone Ranger's nephew's horse?" Mayvee continued, "I've always wondered if that was just some random question the scriptwriters came up with…or if it's based on something factual."

Kord's gorgeous smile spread across his handsome face as he rubbed his hands together in a gesture of triumph.

"Well, here you go," he began. "The Lone Ranger's nephew's horse really was named Victor," Kord said.

"What?" Mayvee exclaimed with an amused giggle. "The Lone Ranger really did have a nephew?"

"Yep," Kord confirmed. "The Lone Ranger's nephew was named Dan Reid Jr., and his horse really was named Victor. He was sired by Silver, the Lone Ranger's horse." He paused, grinning with mischief and adding, "*Victor* was sired by Silver, that is—not Dan."

Mayvee laughed, rolled her eyes, and smacked Kord playfully on one very solid shoulder. "I know that, you dork!" Yet nodding, she admitted, "I didn't know that the nephew thing was true though." She looked at him with one eyebrow quizzically arched. "And how on earth did you know that anyway? Google?"

Kord shrugged. "Nope, though I'm sure it's there. I know because my grandpa was a huge Lone Ranger fan. I used to watch the old TV reruns with him, and he had every book imaginable on the subject. I even dressed up as the Lone Ranger one year for Halloween, but only the old people really knew who I was."

Mayvee laughed as uncontrollable delight bubbled up in her. She could just imagine Kord dressed up as a little version of the Lone Ranger; he must've been adorable!

"How cute!" she exclaimed. "And I'm so impressed with your Lone Ranger knowledge, as well as your movie trivia trunk of tricks."

"Thank you," Kord teased. "I try." His smile broadened again. "Hey, you never yodeled for me! You owe me some yodeling."

"What?" Mayvee exclaimed. "Heck no!"

"Oh, come on, Mayvee," Kord begged, however. "There's no one here but me. Come on."

"No way! It's embarrassing!" she squealed.

"How can it be embarrassing?" he countered. "Come on, just a few yodels, and I'll let you off the hook."

Mayvee's eyebrows arched. "And what do I get in return?" she asked.

Kord sighed, seeming pensive for a moment. Then he answered, "I'll tell you something about myself…something I'm really embarrassed about and that very few people know. In fact, now that I think about it, only me and my doctor know about it."

Instantly Mayvee's curiosity was piqued. "Really? You promise?"

Kord nodded. "I do. I'll tell you about it— something only me and my doctor know—if you yodel for me. And I want the song from the movie, the goat song they sing during the creepy puppet show part."

"Okay then," Mayvee agreed. "But you promise you'll tell me afterward?"

"I promise," Kord chuckled.

In truth, Mayvee couldn't believe she'd agreed to yodel, even a little bit, in front of Kord. After all, this was a guy she wanted to impress—not drive away with a goofy talent usually only performed by desperate beauty pageant contestants.

"Okay, but I might stink at it because I'm so nervous. And I really do yodel the yodeling parts…not just sing them," Mayvee warned him.

"Don't be nervous," Kord said. "It's just me."

He settled back in his chair, folded his arms across his broad chest, and nodded that she should begin.

Rolling her eyes in disgust with herself for getting roped into yodeling (not to mention singing too) in front of Kord, Mayvee inhaled a deep breath and began.

It had been a while since she'd yodeled at all, let alone sung "The Lonely Goatherd," but somehow she managed to pull off a few verses before stage fright completely won her over.

"Awesome!" Kord exclaimed, wholeheartedly applauding her from his weathered old lawn chair. He laughed, continued to clap, and again exclaimed, "Awesome! Seriously, that's the most awesome thing I've ever heard!"

"Yeah, I'm sure," Mayvee said, blushing. "Right up there with a Mariah Carey concert, right?"

But Kord was undaunted, and as his blue-green eyes lit up with admiration, he reiterated, "No, seriously, that was incredible! I love that!" He chuckled for a few more moments and then said, "Do it again."

"No!" Mayvee playfully argued. "Believe me, that's enough humiliation for me to last quite a while."

"Oh, come on, Mayvee," Kord almost begged.

"No way," she firmly said, however. "Now tell me this deep, dark, embarrassing thing that only you and your doctor know about."

Kord exhaled, as if trying to rally the courage to tell her, and Mayvee wondered if maybe it really was something serious.

"Well, I'll just say it. I'm missing a toenail," he almost mumbled.

"What?" Mayvee exclaimed, almost laughing out loud at the same time.

"It's true," he said, nodding to assure her he was being honest. "Last year I dropped an acrylic tank on my foot and messed up the nail bed of my left big toe. The doctor suggested I just have the entire nail bed removed, and so I did. So now…now I just have a toe there…no toenail."

Instantly, Mayvee burst into giggles. "Are you kidding me?" she asked him through her giggling. "That's your big, embarrassing secret?"

Kord chuckled. "Well, I really wanted to hear you yodel, and it was the only thing I could think of that I'm pretty much mortified about and that I was brave enough to let you know about me."

"I totally got the screws on this one, buddy!" Mayvee scolded, slapping his arm again. "Yodeling for toenail info? I'm such a patsy!"

"Hey, Mayvs."

Mayvee turned to see Josh approaching from the rear of the tree lot. He had a brown lunch bag in his hand and looked upset. In the next moment, Mayvee saw exactly why Josh looked so upset: Nick was approaching with him!

"Hey, Josh," Mayvee greeted. "What's going on?" she asked, glancing to Nick.

"Um, Mom thought you guys might like to have some of her toffee bar cookies she made today," Josh stammered. "And…um…Nick saw me coming in the back entrance. He says he just wanted to grab a tree real quick."

Mayvee accepted the brown bag of cookies as Josh handed it to her. She was glad that Kord instantly stood up from his chair, even before she did.

"What do you really want, man?" Kord asked Nick.

Nick's eyes narrowed. He looked Kord up and down, sneered, and said, "I didn't come to see you."

Kord stepped toward Nick.

"But what *do* you want, Nick?" Mayvee asked. "You don't need a tree. You've never needed a tree."

"I actually stopped by to see you, Mayvee," Nick admitted. "I wanted to see if you'd go with me to the firm's Christmas party next Friday. Everyone's been asking about you. And I thought it would be fun to go together."

"I'm sorry, Mayvee," Josh said, frowning. Her little brother looked worried, and Mayvee was even more frustrated with Nick's presence because of it.

"It's not your fault, Josh," Mayvee said. "Nick's just bugged because he saw me and Kord at the mall yesterday and—"

"So do you want to go or not, Mayvs?" Nick interrupted.

"No. I do not want to go, Nick," Mayvee firmly stated. "I don't want to go anywhere with you ever again. And you're only here because of your ego anyway. You saw Kord and me yesterday, and it reminded you of something you can't have…and that's why you're here now. So just go. You'll find another dumb blonde soon enough, and your tender little ego will be all better."

"You do need to leave, man," Kord said, taking another step toward Nick.

"Yeah. I'll call the cops if you don't, Nick," Josh said.

Mayvee could tell that Kord's presence helped Josh in standing up to Nick.

"You shut up," Nick said to Josh. He reached out and shoved the teenager, making him stumble backward.

"Okay, that's it," Kord growled. Reaching out, he took hold of Nick's coat lapels and started pushing him back. "Get out of here. You're trespassing."

"I'm not trespassing," Nick argued. "The kid let me in!"

Forcibly turning Nick around, Kord took hold of the back of his coat collar and shoved him toward the back exit.

"Get your hands off me, loser!" Nick shouted.

But Kord could feel his temper rising to an even higher degree, so he kept pushing Nick toward the back gate. Josh and Mayvee were with him, and once he reached the exit, he gave the guy one more hard shove to send him stumbling out through the open gates.

"Go home, man," Kord told him. "You're done here…for good."

But somewhere between the fire pit and the back exit of the tree lot, Nick had begun feeling his oats.

Turning to face Kord, Nick shoved him. "Who are you to tell me what to do, man? And why don't you let me give you some advice." He pointed to Mayvee. "The girl is a goody-goody. She don't put out anything. So if you're thinking you're going to get lucky by—"

Kord's fist was stinging from the punch before he'd even realized he'd thrown it. But Nick Stevens sitting on his butt—looking dazed, confused, and rubbing his jaw—was further proof to Kord that his protective instincts toward Mayvee really had kicked in.

"You hit me, man! I'll sue your ass!" Nick shouted.

"You're trespassing, man," Kord calmly reminded. "You'll be lucky if the Ashton family doesn't sue yours first. Now get outta here."

"You picked a real winner this time, Mayvee," Nick growled as he struggled to get to his feet.

Kord looked to Mayvee, relieved when she smiled at him and said, "Why yes, I did, Nick." She looked at Nick as Josh closed the gate, chained it, and secured it with a padlock. "Merry Christmas," she added.

Kord inhaled a deep breath in an effort to calm himself. Exhaling, he raked a hand back through his hair.

He'd lost his cool—really lost his cool—but he was pretty certain by the way Mayvee was looking at him that she didn't mind.

"It might be a good time for you to run on into the sales center, Josh," Mayvee said to her brother.

"I'm sorry, Mayvee," Josh began. "I didn't know what to do. Even though I knew you wouldn't want to see him, and—"

"It's all right," Mayvee reassured her brother, giving him a warm hug and an affectionate kiss on the cheek. "I know you were between a rock and a hard place. No worries, okay? Just grab a few of mom's cookies and chill for a while, okay?"

"Okay," Josh said, nodding. He offered a hand to Kord. "Thanks, man," he said. As Kord shook Josh's hand, Josh added, "And by the way, that was awesome!"

Kord grinned a bit and nodded, saying, "Thanks."

"You guys have fun," Josh said. Pausing and smiling at Mayvee with a mischievous expression on his face, Josh added, "See you later…Dagwood."

Josh hurried off then, and Mayvee thought she'd burst with her impatience in wanting him to be inside the sales center so she could be alone with Kord once more.

As Josh closed the sales center door behind him, Kord turned to Mayvee, looking not so much different from a little boy who thought he was about to get scolded.

"So…do you think I'm a total jerk?" Kord asked.

But if there was one thing Mayvee did *not* think Kord Derringer was, it was any kind of a jerk. She thought he was wonderful, gallant, tough, handsome, and her very own Mr. Right.

Therefore, taking hold of the front of his coat, she raised herself on her tiptoes, kissed him squarely on the mouth, and confessed, "I think you're hot, handsome, and heroic."

Kord grinned, and Mayvee quivered with satisfaction as his arms encircled her waist—as he pulled her against him and gazed down into her eyes.

"So you're not mad at me for taking a swing at your old boyfriend?" he asked.

"Not at all," Mayvee admitted. "In fact, I found it very…attractive."

Kord chuckled and then pressed a lingering kiss to her lips.

"So," she began as she gazed up at him, "wanna go back, sit by the fire, and have some cookies with me?"

Kord grinned. "Okay," he said. "And after that, why don't you let me work on getting that sap off your lips…and onto mine?"

Mayvee didn't speak her answer—she kissed it. As Kord's head descended toward hers, she met his commanding kiss with a passionate one of her own. And as their mouths blended in mutual adulation, a zinging so powerful that it nearly knocked her off her feet began ricocheting throughout her body and in her mind.

This is what I want from love, Mayvee thought as she stood wrapped in Kord's powerful arms there in the Christmas tree lot. *Comfort, security, shared interests, laughter, flirtation, and passion—a melding of souls. And this is the man I'm meant to have that love with.*

Mayvee had known Kord, what, a week maybe? She was too caught up in the impassioned cocoon of bliss into which Kord's kisses were weaving her to think clearly about how long she'd known him. But her soul felt as if she'd known him forever—and that was what mattered.

"I'm the one, you know," Kord mumbled against her mouth.

"What?" Mayvee asked, still reeling from her own thoughts and the enchantment Kord was winding around her.

Kord gazed down into her eyes, his own smoldering with desire—bright with affection and love.

"I'm the one…your Mr. Right, Mayvee," he explained.

Mayvee smiled and felt tears welling in her eyes. "I know," she whispered. "I know."

And when Kord kissed Mayvee again—as tears of joy escaped her eyes, trickling over her cheeks—frost began to fall, drifting through the cold night air from the heavens, just as if a black velvet pouch of midnight had opened, spilling a million tiny diamonds over the ideally romantic world of the Christmas tree lot.

EPILOGUE

"I love this part!" Mayvee exclaimed as she cuddled closer to her husband on the bed.

Kord chuckled, "Me too. The Xs over the eyes of the creeping marauders after Ralphie shoots them cracks me up."

"I know, right?" Mayvee agreed as she watched the young hero in *A Christmas Story* skillfully wield his Red Ryder 200-shot range model air rifle in defending off imaginary criminals.

She took a bite of one of the toffee bar cookies her mom and dad had dropped off earlier in the day. "Mmmmm!" she sighed. "I swear, I can never make these as good as Mom's."

Kord took a bite of the cookie she held. "They taste exactly like yours," he told her.

"I don't know," Mayvee mumbled, however.

Kord reached over to the plate sitting on the bed next to him. The remains of his Dagwood sandwich—a couple of pieces of lettuce, a corner off a slice of cheese, and a small piece of salami—lay on the plate, and he picked up the piece of cheese and popped it into his mouth.

Smiling at Mayvee, he said, "Nothing like watching Ralphie try to get a Red Ryder BB gun, enjoying a Dagwood sandwich, and holding my beautiful Blondie on a cold winter's night."

Mayvee giggled. "It's an epic first anniversary date, isn't it?" She kissed Kord on the mouth—lingered in gazing into his beautiful blue-green eyes.

She couldn't believe it had been a year—an entire year since Kord had proposed to her after knowing her less than a week—a year since they'd had their Christmas Eve wedding only three weeks later.

Mayvee thought back to the day, the very moment, Kord had walked onto Ashtons' Christmas Tree Lot. She remembered the way her brother Craig had been teasing her about possibly finding her Dagwood (a.k.a. her one true love) that very day and only moments before Kord had appeared.

She thought about decorating Kord's grandparents' tree, about their shopping date to the mall, and Kord's sending Nick sprawling to the ground with one swift punch. Through all of it—every hour of those first few days with Kord—Mayvee had known Kord was the one her heart and soul needed and had been waiting to find.

Mayvee also thought back on her mother's astonishment when Kord had come to her asking permission to marry Mayvee after less than a week of their knowing each other. She remembered the Skype meeting with her father and how her father had told her that he trusted Mayvee to make wise decisions and that if Mayvee felt Kord was the man she wanted to marry, then she should marry him.

It had all been a whirlwind after that—the wedding plans. It had been a small wedding, the kind both Mayvee and Kord wanted, a Christmas Eve wedding and Christmassy, very well-attended reception to follow—a Christmas Eve that seemed, even then, like a dream world, overflowing with flocked Christmas trees, white twinkle lights, and red-and-white peppermint candy canes, pine boughs and holly, poinsettias and red mums, ham and warm bread to eat, and Christmas cookies with sparkling colored sugar spread over them. Furthermore, Mayvee had never known anyone else in all her life that had actually had Santa Claus attend their reception and distribute little brown bags filled with tangerines, nuts, and candy to all the guests. But the jolly old elf had attended theirs—her and Kord's.

"What are you thinking about?" Kord asked, drawing Mayvee's attention back to the present.

Mayvee smiled and snuggled close to her husband. She sighed and answered, "You…and how much I love you."

Kord chuckled. "Even though I nominated us to spend the night at the tree lot on our first anniversary, instead of whisking you away to some swanky hotel for a romantic evening?"

Mayvee laughed. "Especially for that!" she assured him. She kissed his warm and delicious mouth. "To me, this is the most romantic place we could be."

Kord quirked one eyebrow. "In the back room of the tree lot sales center, watching Christmas movies and eating your mom's cookies?"

"Yes," she answered. "And don't play dumb with me, Mr. Derringer. You planned this because you already *knew* that this is exactly my idea of romance."

Kord kissed Mayvee—a long, slow, moist, and heated kiss.

"You got me," he mumbled against her mouth. He kissed her once more before asking, "Hey, Blondie. Wanna pause the movie and make out for a while?"

Mayvee sighed with satisfaction in anticipation, picked up the remote control, and clicked the power off button. "Of course," she sighed. But as a thought struck her then, a quiet giggle escaped her.

"What's so funny?" Kord asked as he laid his wife back in the bed and hovered over her a moment.

"I was just thinking," Mayvee said as Kord scattered caressive kisses over her neck. "Do you think anybody in all the world would ever even begin to imagine that two people who were so destined to fall in love and be together, the way we were, would meet on Black Friday at a Christmas tree lot?"

Kord smiled. "I suppose stranger things have happened," he said.

"Like what?" Mayvee teased.

Kord's smile faded a bit, even as his eyes sparked with deeply felt emotion.

"Like you actually loving me," he said.

Mayvee's own eyes filled with the moisture born of tender yet profound love. "It's the easiest, most natural thing I've ever known."

"Merry Christmas, my beautiful Christmas tree lot girl," Kord said.

"Merry Christmas, my hot, handsome hero," Mayvee whispered in return.

And as the fading scent of pine still breathed a little from the boughs hanging from the ceiling, as hot chocolate on the nightstand cooled around its peppermint stick stirrer, and as frost began to brush its delicate stencils of crystal lace on the window panes, a romance that began on a Christmas tree lot burned as warm and as passionate as ever did any hearth fire.

AUTHOR'S NOTE

It's been said that all books are somewhat autobiographical. And after finishing this book, I'm more of a believer in that fact than even I was before!

One of my closest friends read *Romance at the Christmas Tree Lot* chapter by chapter as I wrote it. She gives me a short feedback after reading each chapter, and after reading Chapter Seven, this is what she e-mailed to me: "Every time I read one of your books, I see people in your family through the characters you're describing and writing about. In this one, I see YOU!!" And she's right! Of course, I had to skim back through the first seven chapters to see what she was talking about—to try and figure out how I'd managed to be so transparent in this story—but all that did was solidify the facts that, boy, oh boy, does she know me, and, boy, oh boy, is this book me!

I love Christmas! Of course, as you well know, I love autumn too—but autumn is a season whereas Christmas is an event—a time, a holiday. There's

Christmas, and there's winter, and although they go hand in hand, there is a difference. I'm not the biggest fan of winter, although I do enjoy the change to cold weather for a while and would never want to do without it, but it's Christmas that I love. I love the Christmas trees, the holly and pine, the twinkling lights, the shiny glass ornaments, the nutcrackers, the Christmas movies, and vintage Christmas TV specials. I love the way so many people are happier and thinking of others more than themselves. I love the Christmas cards and family photos—the homemade fudge, posole, tamales, avocado dip, and candy canes. I love the hot chocolate, the sewing, the gluing, the door-ditching, the wrapping of gifts, the Christmas caroling, and having so many plates of Christmas cookies from friends and neighbors sitting on the counter that I feel like I might throw up! I love Santa Claus and gingerbread men, elves and snowmen, and even snow. I *love* it all!

But above all else, I love what the season celebrates—the birth of our Savior, Jesus Christ. I love the stable scenes and nativities that depict the event of all events. I love that people do seem more thoughtful of one another, more giving, more *for*giving, and a little more loving overall. And that's why, for me, the celebration of Christmas and what it truly is begins in...oh, I'd say about February. Believe me, I get a lot of guff for being a year-round Christmaser. But I don't care! Because to me, the Spirit of Christmas should be a constant thing—thoughts of our Savior, loving and understanding and doing for each other. To me, it shouldn't be twenty-five days of the year; it should be always.

And I think maybe that's why my friend sees so much of me in this book—because it incorporates so many of the things I feel *all* the time, you know? Shoot, if I thought I could get away with it, I'd be sending Christmas gifts throughout the whole year! Actually, it's probably good then that Kevin keeps me grounded a bit on that part of it; he just helps me keep a level, realistic handle on gift-giving—sometimes. ☺

Anyway, many of the experiences and feelings I incorporated in this non-stressful, *not* overly dramatic, sweet Christmas romance are literally from me—my experiences, my feelings, and my need for something soothing, calm, and fluffily fun at this time of year when so many people press so much upon us. My hope is that you sat down in front of your Christmas tree or your fireplace (or, ideally, both), sipped a big, steaming mug of Stephen's candy cane cocoa, and enjoyed a few hours of respite through reading Kord and Mayvee's story. I hope it made you want to hug a veteran and thank him for his service, to smile at a little old lady and tell her she looks pretty today. I hope it made you want to eat breakfast for supper and have a Christmas tree in your bedroom (assuming you don't already). And I hope it made you feel closer to me as your friend. Merry Christmas! And God bless us, every one!

Love,
Marcia Lynn McClure

Romance at the Christmas Tree Lot Trivia Snippets

Snippet #1—Our little family has always had a fresh-cut Christmas tree. We had our favorite Christmas tree lot in the early years of our marriage, and our two oldest kids have some fond and funny memories of those trips to the Christmas tree lot in Albuquerque. However, our youngest son's first memories of our family Christmas tree outings revolve around a wonderful little place in Ferndale, Washington. This was a "cut-your-own" tree lot, and our little family would march out into a field of pines, select a tree, and then watch as Kevin cut it down himself. In fact, it's the sales center at that Ferndale tree lot that inspired Ashtons' Christmas Tree Lot in this book. That beloved Christmas tree lot in Ferndale did indeed have a rustic little sales center building, where the owners provided hot chocolate and candy canes for patrons. And although Astons' Christmas Tree Lot was even more pampering of their customers, it's the Ferndale lot that was lingering in my mind whenever I was writing about Ashtons'.

Snippet #2—I can't even remember how old I was—actually, I can't even remember how *young* I was—when I first started reading comic strips. In our family, "the funnies," as they were called when I was little, were the best part of the newspaper, and I can remember reading them way, way, way back. I know I was reading them on my own by about second grade, and one of my favorites was *Blondie*. I didn't know the history of the *Blondie* comic strip back then; I just knew her husband, Dagwood, was the funny guy and always making sandwiches that were seemingly several feet high. I grew up with many of the classics, and I had my own favorites; *Peanuts*, *Li'l Abner*, and *Family Circus*. By the time I was a young teenager, I was into *For Better or Worse*. But it was the *Calvin and Hobbes* years I truly loved. Oh, how I still miss *Calvin and Hobbes*! I grew to love *Baby Blues*, *Zits*, and especially *Foxtrot* and others over the years and actually subscribed to the newspaper for most of my married life simply so I could have the daily comics. So over the past probably forty years, I've read comics—including *Blondie*—and a few years back I can across a book that was basically a history of the strip. It was very enlightening! Seems that the comic strip began in the dailies in 1930, with Blondie Boopadoop—a pretty, free-spirited flapper girl. Three years later, Blondie married Dagwood Bumstead, who was disinherited by his wealthy father for marrying Blondie. But Dagwood didn't care, and he and Blondie (who morphed into a beautiful, sweet housewife and mother) have remained happy in wedded bliss for over eighty years since! Anyway, the fact that Mayvee is a blonde made Blondie Boopadoop Bumstead pop into my mind when I was writing the first chapter of this book. And, after all, who's Blondie without her Dagwood and his sandwich, right? And that's how another piece of nostalgia from my childhood and past made it into the story of Kord and Mayvee's romance.

Snippet #3—Now, I know that this next snippet addresses a very sensitive subject—Black Friday! Yikes! There are those who love it and those who hate it and those who are indifferent to it. Admittedly, I'm on

Kord's side where Black Friday is concerned—meaning I'm not a fan of Black Friday, do enjoy Cyber Monday, but also believe in miracles like Kord himself experienced (meeting his one true love on Black Friday). I won't go into the particulars or stand up too long on my soapbox in regard to all the ranting about "the commercialism of Christmas." I'll just say that Kord's feelings of anxiety in regard to Black Friday mirror my own. We're both anti-Black Friday-ers—especially when Black Friday starts on Thanksgiving Thursday! Ha ha!

Snippet #4—I'm not sure you're aware of this, but I *love* Christmas trees! Here's me (above) decorating our family tree in December of 1972. I have loved Christmas trees as far back as I can remember, and I know this is a passion many of my readers share with me. There's just something about them that soothes my spirit and gives me hope—makes me sort of tingle with joy. So yes, admittedly, Mayvee's moonlighting job of decorating Christmas trees is based on the fact that I love Christmas trees to such an infinite depth that I'm not sure anyone could ever understand it, you know? Along with that, I do have a plan to one day have a rustic cabin interior, Christmas themed guest room! I have it all planned out—even have the signs already made to hang above the door. But right now, I'm not willing to give up one of my other themed bedrooms to do it—not yet, at least. But one day, "The Cozy Cabin" themed room will join my "The Pumpkin Patch," "An Autumn Haven," "A long time ago, in a galaxy far, far away…" and "Romance, Cherries, and Chocolate" bedrooms as part of our home. I can't wait!

Snippet #5—Why yes, I most certainly *do* enjoy incorporating elderly characters in my stories—in case you haven't noticed. To me, elderly people (especially one's own grandparents) are a treasure! They're wise beyond comprehension, experienced, and most of the time hold to a moral standard and level of etiquette the world is sadly lacking these days. I find that they own life histories that are so astounding and awe-inspiring—filled with integrity, humility, and patriotism. I know that my own character is improved by heeding the guidance of those generations who have endured things that I often can't even imagine. It makes me a better person. If you really want to build your character and work on gaining a knowledge that only a lifetime of experience can offer, then take those moments to sit down and visit with elderly folks as often as your time will allow.

Snippet #6—Once I had four betta fish and one goldfish, all in separate containers, and I *loved* them! I've always dreamed of having the time, knowhow, and tenacity to own a really high-end aquarium. However, after watching what my friend's husband went through to care for his, I realized I just couldn't hack it. And then the Animal Planet channel came up with *Tanked*— *love* it! Dream about it! Would have to be richer than Donald Trump to afford to have it be maintained. And so I'll stick with betta fish—except that I had an incident a few years back while cleaning one of my betta containers. Let's just say I poured the wrong cup of old betta fish water down the garbage disposal and have been traumatized ever since. (His name was Earl, by the way.) Thus, I'll leave the aquariums to people like Kord and the guys on *Tanked*.

Snippet #7—When I was eight years old, the 1965 movie version of the *Sound of Music* was rereleased and my Auntie (pronounced AWN-tee) took me to see it. It was an epic, life-changing experience for me. Not only did I think Captain Von Trapp was *totally* handsome and *so* romantic in that scene where he and Maria *finally* confess their love for each other (swoon), but the music and songs were incredible! It was those songs that made me want to sing just like Julie Andrews, and from a very young age I would impersonate her—especially during "The Lonely Goatherd" song. My mother had always been a fan of Slim Whitman, who was a profoundly gifted yodeler, so yodeling wasn't new to me. I'd grown up listening to Slim Whitman records (especially my mom's favorite song in the world, Slim's version of "Indian Love Call"), so I was already a pretty good little yodeler by the time I was eight and first saw the *Sound of Music*. But once I added "The Lonely Goatherd" to my repertoire, look out world, here I came! I don't sing enough to yodel well anymore, and it's true what they say—if you don't use it, you lose it. After all, the human voice is an instrument, and if you don't keep it cared for and use it often…well, let's just say, your yodel skidooddles. But there's even more to Mayvee's yodeling than my own history. While writing this book, I was over at my son, daughter-in-law, and granddaughter's house one evening when my son hurried into his daughter's bedroom and came back with a gift my granddaughter had received from her other grandma. It was a puppet that looked like a silly goat, and when you made its mouth move, it sang and yodeled "The Lonely Goatherd" from the *Sound of Music*! What an awesome novelty item, right? I loved the puppet and have since given one to my Auntie, who introduced me to the *Sound of Music* in the first place, and one to my BFF who is now a grandma too! I mean, grandma toys that are unique and special are a must. And there you have the inspirations for Mayvee's yodeling "The Lonely Goatherd."

Snippet #8—Years and years back, I was doing a bit of Christmas shopping in Wal-Mart. While browsing around in the jewelry/wristwatch section, I noticed a little old lady digging through her coin purse. She had a little item in her hand (I really do think it was earrings), and after digging in her coin purse a moment, she returned the item to the hook and moved on. Even now, today, sitting here writing about it, my heart is aching, my stomach feels nauseous, and my eyes are watering with hurt and disappointment for the little lady. At that time, I didn't have any cash on my person, at all. (This was back when people wrote checks for everything. Some of you may have to look that up to know what I mean. Wink-wink!) I was distraught about what to do. I didn't want to offer to pay for the item for her and embarrass her, and I had a couple of my children with me, and they were getting tired of errands, you know? And so I did nothing—nothing at all—and I've been sick to my stomach ever since. I think very, very often, and especially every holiday season, about my sweet little maternal grandmother, Opal States. My grandpa (her husband) passed away in 1984, and I know it broke her heart in so many ways. She was never the same, even though she'd struggled with health problems for years—and I can still see her digging through her "pocketbook" that was filled with gum, matchbooks, Kleenex, and her pretty, very feminine cigarette case, looking for change to pay for something (though I don't remember what at this moment). I know how giving she was, how much she wanted to give, and how fixed her income was, and she's one reason I have that tender spot for little old ladies, you know? She was also very thoughtful about the gifts and cards she gave. I remember being with her one time as she was browsing for a card for a young relative. She picked up one card and read the sentiment aloud to me. It was something like, "To a wonderful young man. You are so kind to me, dear, so considerate, so sweet and loving." Grandma promptly closed the card, said, "Well, that's certainly not true!" and continued looking for another, more appropriate card. I still crack up out loud when I think of her in that moment. Even at the time, I figured she didn't realize she'd said what she'd said aloud—she was never cruel. But let me tell you this: I've never purchased another mushy card since if I didn't sincerely feel the sentiment written in it for the person the card was for! Little old ladies and weathered old war veterans—two of my favorite things, two things that tenderize my heart exactly as if someone were striking it with a meat mallet.

Snippet #9—When I was about four years old, I got so impatient waiting for Christmastime to come that in July I started gathering pretty rocks and wrapping them up in Christmas wrapping paper to give as gifts. Hmmm, now that I think about, I still like to wrap Christmas gifts starting in July. Mayvee is a kindred spirit of mine in that she started wrapping rocks in wildly delighted anticipation of Christmas gift-giving as a toddler too.

Snippet #10—I think I've mentioned this to you before, but there was a time when I could recite the entire script of the now classic Christmas movie *A Christmas Story*. *A Christmas Story* is one of my favorite movies ever, and after I had my first baby and was going through the postpartum blues, I would pop in the old VHS tape and play *A Christmas Story* over and over and over all day long as I cleaned house and cuddled with my baby. I just liked having the company of my favorite movie playing—just until Kevin got home and I felt more self-confident and secure as a new mother. So seriously, I really could have recited the whole movie to you then. And crossword puzzle question about the Lone Ranger's nephew's horse? I always wondered if the Lone Ranger really did have a nephew and if his horse's name really was Victor. And so when writing this story, I decided to do a little research. And guess what? The Lone Ranger really did have a nephew who really did have a horse named Victor! The Lone Ranger's nephew was Dan Reid Jr., though the world doesn't seem to know Dan's true first name. It seems his mother was tragically killed in an Indian attack, and Dan was taken in by Grandma Frisbee, who then raised him. He got the name Dan from a locket that his mother had worn. Dan Jr. eventually rode Victor, the son of Silver. Are you amazed at my ability to dig up such important, life-changing facts? Well, if so, here's another one: After nearly thirty years of referring to the bully in *A Christmas Story* as "Scott Fargus," imagine my surprise when my daughter (also a discoverer of incredibly life-changing information) informed me that the bully's name is actually Scut Farkus! I mean, who knew? Anyway, the Lone Ranger's nephew's horse really is named Victor, and people apparently used to name their boys Scut. Information you couldn't go on living a full life without, right?

Snippet #11—Many of you have heard the story of how my husband, Kevin, and I met. And though I've said this before, I'll say it again—because it does apply to this story. The moment I met Kevin—even before that, the moment I saw him—I knew I was in love with him. I also knew that I would marry him, though I doubted it could really happen at first. I mean, he was literally the handsomest young man I had ever seen! I knew when I met him that he was my one and only Mr. Right. Thus, as you may already know, though I don't believe it happens for everyone, I do absolutely believe in love at first sight. Even more than that, I believe in "knowing" at first sight. It's rare, but it does happen—a man and woman knowing the moment they meet that they are meant to be together. And if my own story of finding my Mr. Perfectly Imperfect dreamboat isn't enough for you, I also have a friend whose story goes like this: She went on a date with a guy on one New Year's Eve about thirty years ago. On New Year's Day (the very next day), they went on their second date and proposed to each other then and there! They've been married ever since, weathering life's blisses and blessings, heartaches and elations. It really does happen, knowing you've found "the one" at the moment you meet him—just the way Kord and Mayvee did.

Snippet #12—And now, last but certainly not least, I'd like to share Mayvee's mom's Toffee Bar Cookie recipe with you! It's my mom's recipe too—a family favorite—and one of the only cookies my husband actually loves. My mom used to make them every year for Kevin as her Christmas gift to him, so you see it's extra special to us! I hope you enjoy it!

Toffee Bar Cookies

Ingredients:
1 cup butter (*do not use* shortening!)
1 cup brown sugar
1 egg yolk
1 teaspoon vanilla
2 cups flour
1 milk chocolate bar (6 oz.)
1 cup finely chopped pecans

Cream together butter and brown sugar. Mix in egg yolk and vanilla. Gradually add flour, and mix well.

Press batter in lightly greased glass 9×13 pan. Bake at 325°F for 25 to 30 minutes until crust is golden brown.

Remove from oven and immediately break up chocolate over top. When chocolate is soft, use a butter knife to evenly spread chocolate over top of crust. Sprinkle on nuts.

Allow to cool some, but cut while still warm. *These need several hours for the chocolate to then set up before serving.

Note: The truth is Mom has the best recipes ever! This was a staple at our house during the Christmas holidays, especially on Christmas Eve!

Merry Christmas! From Marcia Lynn McClure—
A Lover of Christmas

And now, enjoy the first chapter of
**THE ROMANCING OF
EVANGELINE IPSWICH,**
the third book in the
Three Little Girls Dressed in Blue Trilogy
by Marcia Lynn McClure.

CHAPTER ONE

"Another letter to your friend?" Mrs. Perry asked

Evangeline nodded, smiling as she handed the letter to Mrs. Perry to post. "Yes. I try to respond as quickly as I'm able."

"You're a sweetheart, Evangeline Ipswich. No doubt about it," Mrs. Perry commented. "And how is your friend doin'? Bein' that she's expectin' her baby soon and all."

Evangeline frowned, wondering whether she should even share her knowledge of her friend Jennie's condition with Mrs. Perry. After all, though Mrs. Perry and her husband owned the general store in Meadowlark Lake and were quite good friends to Evangeline and her family, Sophia Perry didn't know Jennie personally. She paused then in answering, uncertain of the propriety of discussing Jennie's situation with a stranger to her.

However, Evangeline's concern for Jennie, coupled with her need for reassurance, made the determination for her, and she answered, "Not as well as we would all like to hear."

Mrs. Perry frowned, prodding, "Oh?"

Evangeline shook her head, sending a stray strand of raven hair that had escaped a hairpin cascading down over one shoulder. "No. In fact, the doctor has urged her to bedrest for the remainder of her time."

"Oh dear!" Mrs. Perry exclaimed in a whisper. It was obvious the woman's concern was sincere, and Evangeline was glad she'd chosen to confide in her regarding Jennie's state.

"Yes. It's very worrisome," Evangeline continued. "In fact, Jennie as has asked me to…" She paused, for she couldn't reveal Jennie's request to Mrs. Perry—not when she hadn't even informed her own family about it.

"She asked you to what, dear?" Mrs. Perry asked, patiently waiting for Evangeline's response.

"To…to write to her as often as I can," Evangeline answered.

Mrs. Perry smiled and nodded. "I can well imagine what a great comfort your letters are to her. Why, I was laid up in bed for near to six weeks when I was expectin' my Culver. And he was a big baby when he finally came too—near to nine pounds, Culver was. And I know letters from my sister…well, they surely did give me somethin' to look forward to."

"I do hope so," Evangeline sighed. "I mean to say, I'm not even sequestered to bedrest, and I so look forward to each and every one of Jennie's letters."

"With all you've got goin' on to keep you busy, Evangeline Ipswich?" Mrs. Perry laughed. "Why, that baby sister of yours probably keeps you runnin' hither and yon all day, especially now that both your other sisters are married." Mrs. Perry sighed. "Oh, I've never in all my life seen weddin's as romantic and beautiful as your father's and your two sisters' were. Why, it's been almost a year since Amoretta married that handsome Brake McClendon, hasn't it?" Without waiting for an answer, she prattled, "And your father, the honorable Judge Ipswich, married the beautiful gypsy from the woods, Kizzy. Not to mention Rowdy Gates takin' Calliope to wife just over three months past. And every one of those weddin's was just a dream!"

"Yes," Evangeline agreed, although somewhat disheartenedly. It was true, both of Evangeline's younger blood sisters, Amoretta and Calliope, were married, happily settled in with handsome, loving husbands. Even her own father, Lawson Ipswich, had remarried almost a year before—and to a young and beautiful woman who brought with her an adorable daughter, Shay.

Still, though her joy was overflowing for her sisters and her father, she inwardly worried that she would become the Spinster Ipswich, that no man would ever pursue her—at least, no man that she desired to pursue her.

"I hear Mr. Longfellow has been quite attentive to you, honey," the well-meaning proprietress of the general store ventured. "He's a very handsome man, Evangeline. And those two little girls of his are just as sweet as peaches!"

Evangeline blushed a little and felt her emerald green eyes begin to fill with the excess moisture borne of disappointment. Floyd Longfellow had indeed made no attempt to hide the fact that he was wildly interest in Evangeline. But kind as Floyd was, he was Evangeline's own father's age. And though perhaps that should not have mattered to her, it did. Evangeline had felt the weight of responsibility far too long—often felt older than her mere twenty-two years should have her feel. And she wanted a younger man—a man who did not own the heavy burden of memories of two wives who had passed on to heaven far before their time.

Her own stepmother, Kizzy—the beautiful gypsy woman who had healed her father's heart and married him—was certainly much younger than Evangeline's father. But there was a difference in her own father and Floyd Longfellow. Lawson Ipswich still had a young heart and was strong, handsome, and virile. He flirted and teased his young wife, and Evangeline knew that when Kizzy and her father's new baby arrived in November, her father would be as energetic and as loving to him or her as he ever had been from Evangeline's birth down to having adopted little six-year-old Shay.

She could not think the same of Floyd Longfellow—a lonely, haunted sort of man. Evangeline needed youthfulness. She'd had to grow up too fast and own too much responsibility when her own mother had passed away when she was a girl of only twelve. And Floyd Longfellow had two little girls of his own that needed nurturing and love. And though she wanted children, she wanted children of her own—babies born of love and with a vibrant father.

Therefore, though she felt guilt-ridden for not appreciating the fact that Floyd Longfellow would propose and marry her that very moment if she would only agree to it, she smiled at Mrs. Perry and said, "He's a very kind man, but…but…"

Mrs. Perry smiled with understanding, reached out, and clasped Evangeline's hand in her own. "Floyd *is* a very kind man," she affirmed. "And I'm sure that one day he'll find himself a very kind woman to help him though life." She patted Evangeline's hand and added, "So you let him find that woman one day, and go where your heart leads you, darlin'."

Evangeline sighed with relief. She smiled, thinking how kind Mrs. Perry was—what a dear friend she had become. Sophia Perry was always so kind to everyone, and the merry little lady with the sweet, round face was kindest of all to Evangeline. At least is seemed so to Evangeline. She always felt more cheerful after a visit with Mrs. Perry. She had hair that looked as if it had been spun from cinnamon and sugar and the brightest smile in all of Meadowlark Lake. It was no wonder she made a body feel more hopeful and happy.

"Thank you, Mrs. Perry," Evangeline said in quite gratitude. "I-I struggle so with a feeling of obligation toward the man."

Mrs. Perry sighed. "It's that sackcloth-and-ashes demeanor of his, I'm afraid. Makes a body feel simply miserable and gray and guilty, doesn't it?"

Evangeline giggled. She couldn't help herself in giggling, because Mrs. Perry had expressing Evangeline's feelings exactly. "It does," she admitted.

"And a beautiful young woman like you, Evangeline…you need strength and joy, hope, and a bit more muscle on a man than Floyd Longfellow can provide, I'm afraid," Mrs. Perry offered with a mischievous grin. "It's clear your sisters, Amoretta and Calliope, were both drawn to handsome, muscular men who passionately love them and bathe them in happiness. And you should not relinquish yourself to anything less than what they aspired to, hmm?"

Evangeline nodded, feeling much better than she had when she'd first entered the general store to post her letter to Jennie—much better. Yet she frowned a bit. "The problem is, Mrs. Perry," she began, lowering her voice, "that the only other available young men in town are my sisters' castoffs." She shrugged, adding, "And none of them really interest me even if they weren't."

"Well, don't you give that another worry, sweet pea," Mrs. Perry reassured, patting the back of Evangeline's hand affectionately. "Some tall drink of water will wander on into town one day. It's always the way it seems…least around these parts."

Evangeline watched as Mrs. Perry inked her postmarking stamp and slammed it down on the front of Evangeline's letter to Jennie.

"There we are," she said as she placed the letter to Jennie in a satchel filled with other letters the townsfolk of Meadowlark Lake had written. "Your friend will have her letter in hardly any time at all."

"Thank you, Mrs. Perry," Evangeline said, smiling.

"You're welcome, honey," Mrs. Perry said with a wink. "Now you have yourself a nice afternoon. And tell your sweet step-mamma that I said, hello, all right?"

"I will," Evangeline assured the woman.

Stepping out of the general store, Evangeline glanced around in search of her little sister, Shay. Shay had been Evangeline's near constant companion the past few months—ever since Sheriff Montrose, Judge Ipswich, and Evangeline's newest brother-in-law, Rowdy Gates, had exchanged gunfire with the Morrison brothers' gang of outlaws. It seemed the incident had frightened little Shay Ipswich more than her family had initially realized. Therefore, instead of taking her poor marmalade cat, Molly, for leashed walks on her own, Shay had begun begging Evangeline to accompany her.

"Evie!" Evangeline heard Shay call.

Looking across the street to the diner, Evangeline saw that Shay sat in conversation with Warren Ackerman—a little boy in town just a couple of years older than Shay.

"Warren and me are just sittin' over here talkin'," Shay called. "Is it okay if I stay with Warren a while longer? He say's he'll walk home with me and Molly."

Evangeline giggled as she looked down to where Molly sat looking bored but patient at Shay's feet. She shook her head, as ever astonished at the nonsense the poor old marmalade feline put up with.

"Yes, sweetheart," Evangeline called. Her own smile broadened as Shay's dark eyes lit up with delight. "But don't linger too long, all right? Don't let Kizzy and me start worrying about you."

"I won't," Shay assured her older sister.

Evangeline giggled to herself as she watched Warren Ackerman's face pink up with embarrassment when Shay linked her arm with his. It seemed Shay and Warren had been nearly inseparable at times—ever since they'd played the bride and groom in the Tom Thumb wedding presented to the townsfolk that past summer. They'd become fast friends, and Evangeline was glad her littlest sister didn't want for companionship.

Exhaling a heavy sigh, Evangeline turned toward home. "Even my baby sister has a beau," she mumbled to herself.

Inhaling a deep breath of fresh autumn air, however, Evangeline lifted her chin, straightened her posture, and started for home. After all, now that she'd made her decision, she had so much to do in preparing for her trip. First and foremost was telling her family about her plans.

Evangeline wondered how they would feel about it—about her agreeing to Jennie's request that she come and stay with her until the baby was born sometime near the end of October. She wondered if they'd be upset with her for not having discussed it with them before she'd written to Jennie and promised that she would travel out to help her. Certainly she knew that Shay would be disappointed. Yet Calliope and Rowdy lived so close that Shay would never be too lonesome. And Shay did have her friend Warren to keep her company too. Furthermore, Amoretta and Brake would be moving back to Meadowlark Lake before the snows settled in. So between two older sisters, two brothers-in-law, and her father and mother, Shay would be more than attended to.

Of course, Kizzy was expecting a baby as well, and Evangeline had experienced a measure of guilt about leaving her. Yet Kizzy seemed as robust and as strong as ever. Therefore, Evangeline had little doubt that Kizzy would be fine, and she would have Amoretta and Calliope to watch over her. In any case, Jennie's baby was due near to a month before Kizzy's was. So there would be plenty of time for Evangeline to return home for Thanksgiving and the birth of her new little brother or sister, as well as the Christmas holidays.

Evangeline sighed with self-assurance that going to Jennie was the best venue before her. Jennie needed her help. Her family in Meadowlark Lake did not.

She glanced about then to the beauty of autumn all around her. The trees that dotted the main thoroughfare of Meadowlark Lake were already boasting colorful leaves of crimson and orange and gold. The pumpkins nestled betwixt the vines in the fields on the horizon just beyond town were already a beautiful orange where they lay. No doubt Meadowlark Lake's annual pumpkin parade held on All Hallow's Eve would be a breathtaking sight to behold. At the thought of missing the town's All Hallow's Eve social, a twinge of regret did indeed pinch Evangeline's heart. But Jennie had assured Evangeline that autumn in Red Peak was just as lovely as in any other out west.

Therefore, she sighed with satisfaction in her decision to visit Jennie and continued to amble toward home.

"You're back already, Evie?" Kizzy asked as Evangeline entered the house through the back kitchen door. "I thought you'd linger awhile with Mrs. Perry."

Evangeline smiled as she studied her striking young stepmother a moment. Pregnancy only complimented Kizzy's dark beauty—only made her dark eyes appear more mysterious and her lovely smile more soothing.

"We chatted for bit," Evangeline explained. "But for some reason, I just wanted to get home." She added, "And Shay wanted to stay and play with Warren for a little while. I told her it would be fine. I hope you don't mind."

Kizzy giggled, shaking her head with amusement. "Not at all. Shay certainly is sweet on that little boy, isn't she?"

Evangeline laughed a little as well. "She certainly is," she agreed.

Kizzy smiled at Evangeline and suggested, "Why don't you sit down a bit and keep me company while I finish mixin' this cake for dessert tonight, hmmm?"

"All right," Evangeline agreed. She took a seat at the kitchen table, exhaling a rather weary-sounding sigh as she did so.

Kizzy Ipswich's eyes narrowed as she studied Evangeline. There was a growing unhappiness in Lawson Ipswich's eldest daughter. Kizzy had watched it spread through her countenance for past six months or so, and she sensed what was causing it—though she did not know how to stop it. She knew *what* would stop it but not how to make the *what* happen.

Evangeline's history was somewhat a sad one. Her mother, Lawson's first wife, had passed away when Evangeline was only twelve. And as nearly always happened in such situations, Evangeline began to be the one to care for her two younger sisters, Amoretta and Calliope. Forced into being a woman with responsibility at such a young age had stripped Evangeline of most of the carefree and pleasurable parts of adolescence and young-womanhood. Furthermore, the loss of her mother and consequent load of responsibility had left its mark on her heart and soul as well.

Of course, Amoretta and Calliope were also devastated by the death of their mother. But they had been younger than Evangeline—still children—and had not borne the brunt of effect that Evangeline had. And now Evangeline sat at the kitchen table, knowing that both her younger sisters had met, fallen in love with, and married astonishingly handsome men who were strong, loving, and thoroughly obsessed with their wives. Even her own father had fallen in love with Kizzy—and, in marrying her, acquired another daughter who was young and fresh and vibrant. And there was the baby on the way—another joy her father would know that Evangeline could not yet imagine herself being blessed with.

Oh, the girl wasn't bitter—not in the least of it—a fact that spoke to Kizzy of Evangeline's high character and strong heart. But there had begun a nearly tangible sense of disappointment and heightening unhappiness to settle around her like a veil of lost hope, and it worried Kizzy.

"What's eatin' at your thoughts, Evie?" Kizzy asked then. She chose that moment to finally inquire of Evangeline about her feelings, because the two of them were alone in the house. She knew it would easier for Evangeline to express concerns or deep feelings then, as opposed to when her father and Shay were present.

Evangeline shrugged. "Oh, nothing so much as is worth discussing now, I don't think."

But Kizzy smiled. "Tell me, Evie. What's in your mind?"

Evangeline's heart began to race with anxiety as the idea settled in her that perhaps she should confide in Kizzy. After all, Kizzy was a wise woman—far wiser than most women of her young age. By past experience, Evangeline had come to know that it was often very sensible and helpful to confide in Kizzy. Furthermore, it was well Kizzy knew Evangeline's father and how he would feel and react to certain things.

And so in an instant Evangeline decided to leap and said, "I've written Jennie and told her I would travel to be with her until the baby arrives. She's terribly worried, especially now that the doctor has put her to bed for the remainder of her time. I plan to leave next week—to have someone drive me up to Langtree where I can board the train to Red Peak to be with Jennie."

She watched as Kizzy continued to stir the cake batter in the bowl she had propped in one arm. Her heart hammered with trepidation as she waited for Kizzy's response.

Thankfully, Kizzy responded quickly by smiling and saying, "I think it's a wonderful idea, Evie! You need to get away from Meadowlark Lake for a while, I think. And your friend Jennie…well, it sounds like she certainly needs help, not to mention some extra companionship. I imagine it's quite a miserable thing to be put to bed for over a month."

All at once, Evangeline's heart leapt with excitement. "Oh, Kizzy, really? Do you really think I should go? I mean, I've already written to her and told her that I would, but I've been so afraid to tell everyone…especially Daddy. But if *you* think it's wise for me to go, then all my fears will settled."

Kizzy smiled and nodded her reassurance as she said, "I *do* think you should go, Evie. There's nothing here for you at the moment. You need an adventure of sorts. And though I do admit some concern over the fact that you will be servin' someone again—for it seems you've done that at every turn—I do think you need somethin' different for now." Kizzy paused, quirked one eyebrow, and added, "Now as for your father—mind you, he might not be as sure as I am that you need to go, but I'll explain things to him, and he'll come around. So no worries there. Though I do think you should talk to him right away about it."

"Oh, I will!" Evangeline exclaimed. The joy at knowing Kizzy approved of her decision sparked sheer delight in her at the prospect of leaving Meadowlark Lake for a while and seeing Jennie again. "We were such good friends as girls, Jennie and I," Evangeline told Kizzy. "The fun we used to have!" She giggled and added, "And the mischief we used to get into! I think we must've driven our mothers nearly mad with our antics." She sighed, saddened at the memory of the loss of her mother. "Of course, that was before…before…"

"Before your mother passed away and you stepped into the responsibilities left by her absence," Kizzy finished.

"Yes," Evangeline admitted. Quickly, however, she countered, "Not that I minded at all, Kizzy…truly! I loved caring for Amoretta and Calliope. It's just that…well, I miss being young and carefree the way Jennie and I were when we were children."

"Well, you're still very young, Evangeline Ipswich," Kizzy reminded.

But Evangeline countered, "I'm old enough that Floyd Longfellow thinks I'd make a good mother for his little girls."

Kizzy rolled her eyes and laughed. "Ha! Floyd Longellow doesn't care about you being a mother for his girls. He's just smitten by your youth and beauty, Evangeline. The motherin' of his girls is the last thing on his mind where you're concerned." Kizzy shook her head and said, "And besides, once you're gone off to Red Peak to Jennie, Floyd will start pantin' over Blanche Gardener, Winnie Montrose, or some other pretty young thing in town. So don't let the fact that an older man is sweet on you start you to thinkin' you're too old for the likes of the young bucks." Kizzy smiled and winked at Evangeline. "But I will tell you this," she began. "When the day comes that one of them young bucks comes along and captures your attention, Evie…you're gonna need to let him know he's got it."

"What do you mean?" Evangeline asked—for she was a bit confused by Kizzy's instruction.

"I mean that you're a unique beauty, my darlin'," Kizzy explained, "the kind of beauty that good, humble men are afraid to pursue."

But Evangeline sighed with disagreement. "Now I *know* you and Daddy have been talking about me…because that's what he always tells me."

"Well, he tells you that because it's the truth," Kizzy said. "Men of good character and heroic hearts tend to have very humble souls, Evie. They tend toward thinkin' they're not good enough for a raven-haired beauty with deep emerald eyes and a name like Evangeline Ipswich."

Evangeline giggled and shook her head with amusement. "A raven-haired beauty with deep emerald eyes, am I?"

"Yes. You are," Kizzy confirmed. She inhaled a breath of determination and continued, "For instance, your newest brother-in-law…how long did he pine away after your sister Calliope, thinkin' he wasn't worthy of her, hmmm? A long time, I think. And it's worse with you, because your features are dark and mysterious. It intimidates some men."

As Evangeline's deep emerald eyes met Kizzy deep brown ones, she suddenly understood what Kizzy was expressing. "You're speaking from your own experience, I would guess," she offered.

"Yes," Kizzy answered. "Though I never saw myself as some great beauty—or even a simple beauty. Pshaw, I always said. I think it was merely that I'm dark-haired and dark-eyed, with gypsy blood in my veins that the sort of men I was attracted to never approached me. Still, your father argues otherwise with me." Kizzy smiled, blushed a little, and almost whispered, "But your father wasn't afraid of me…not in any regard." Quickly she added, "Yet I *did* have to encourage him for some reason. And that's why I'm tellin' you, Evie. When there finally arrives a man that captures your eye—and therefore your heart—you must give confidence to him. Let him know that you're wantin' his attention."

Evangeline mulled over what Kizzy had told her, but only for an instant before she said, "Well, that's neither here not there anyway. I'm going up to be with Jennie. And besides. I'm sure there are even fewer eligible young men in Red Peak than there are here in Meadowlark Lake." Evangeline frowned, shook her head, and waved a hand as if dismissing her thoughts. "I need to go to Jennie. That's why I'm going."

"I know," Kizzy said.

Her voice was calming, and Evangeline returned to her feelings of excitement about going to be with Jennie.

"Just do tell your father soon, all right, Evangeline?" Kizzy asked in an almost pleading manner. "You're his eldest daughter, honey. You'll be the one he has the hardest time lettin' go."

Evangeline smiled, again amazed at Kizzy's insight. "I won't wait, Kizzy. I'll tell him tonight…just after dinner."

Kizzy nodded and said, "Thank you, Evie." She giggled then, exclaiming, "Oh, I'm so excited for you! What an adventure it will be, hmm?"

Evangeline laughed at Kizzy's obvious delight in Evangeline's pending trip. For a moment, she wasn't too certain how traveling to help care for a bedridden woman qualified as an adventure, but the more she thought about it as an adventure, the more it felt as if it would be.

Yes, throughout the remainder of the day, Evangeline thought of the traveling on the train from Langtree to Red Peak—of seeing the beautiful red rock Jennie had told her composed the hills and mesas around the town, of witnessing so much in a place she'd never been before. And most of adventurous of all would be the time spent with Jennie. If the delight and exuberance in Jennie's letters to Evangeline was any indication of how thoroughly she had remained the same mischievous, amusing person she had been as a girl, then Evangeline knew that her trip north to see her friend would indeed be the adventure of a lifetime!

To my one and only true, true love…
My husband, Kevin!

ABOUT THE AUTHOR

Marcia Lynn McClure's intoxicating succession of novels, novellas, and e-books—including *Weathered too young*, *Midnight Masquerade*, *The Heavenly Surrender*, and *A Good-Lookin' Man*—has established her as one of the most favored and engaging authors of true romance. Her unprecedented forte in weaving captivating stories of western, medieval, regency, and contemporary amour void of brusque intimacy has earned her the title "The Queen of Kissing."

Marcia, who was born in Albuquerque, New Mexico, has spent her life intrigued with people, history, love, and romance. A wife, mother, grandmother, family historian, poet, and author, Marcia Lynn McClure spins her tales of splendor for the sake of offering respite through the beauty, mirth, and delight of a worthwhile and wonderful story.

BIBLIOGRAPHY

A Bargained-For Bride
Beneath the Honeysuckle Vine
A Better Reason to Fall in Love
The Bewitching of Amoretta Ipswich
Born for Thorton's Sake
The Chimney Sweep Charm
Christmas Kisses
A Crimson Frost
Daydreams
Desert Fire
Divine Deception
Dusty Britches
The Fragrance of her Name
A Good-Lookin' Man
The Haunting of Autumn Lake
The Heavenly Surrender
The Highwayman of Tanglewood
Kiss in the Dark
Kissing Cousins
The Light of the Lovers' Moon
Love Me
The Man of Her Dreams
The McCall Trilogy
Midnight Masquerade
An Old-Fashioned Romance
One Classic Latin Lover, Please
The Pirate Ruse
The Prairie Prince
The Rogue Knight
Romance at the Christmas Tree Lot

CPSIA information can be obtained
at www.ICGtesting.com
Printed in the USA
FSOW04n1719060915
10752FS

9 780991 387892